A
VACATION
TO
KILL
FOR

A VACATION TO KILL FOR

A VINTAGE MYSTERY

EUNICE MAYS BOYD
with
ELIZABETH REED ADEN

Author Photo Credit:

For Elizabeth: James Studios (Madison, WI)

For Eunice – old family photo

First edition

ISBN: 978-1-68512-262-1

Cover art by Laura Duffy Design

This book was professionally typeset on Reedsy.
Find out more at reedsy.com

To my niece Nancy Mays Rademaker and her husband Ted who loved to bicycle through Europe and their children, John, Kirk and Erica.

Reviews for Murder Breaks Trail (1943)

"No scientific sleuthing this, but a blending of clues, coincidences and concentration...A better than most brain workout."—*Kirkus Reviews*

"As pretty, suspenseful and smoothly written a mystery as I've read in a long time."—Chicago *Sun*

"... well-tangled murder plot... Good entertainment."—New York *Herald Tribune*

"An exceptional who-done-it, which won honorable mention in the latest Mary Roberts Rinehart mystery novel contest, has been skillfully built into a book that is hard to put down until the last page"—Philadelphia *Evening Bulletin*

Chapter One

The rain began to fall.

Allegra Tate could hear it pattering on the roof of the motor coach, see it on the road ahead and on the vineyards of Provence. Last night in Nice the moon had been shining on the Cote d'Azure—a gibbous moon. Leaning back in her coach seat, Allegra wished she'd never thought of gibbous. She tried to remind herself that gibbous as applied to the moon bore no relation to gibbet—as applied to the gallows—the structure from which criminals were hung.

What a terrible thought to dredge up on a spectacular trip like this, she thought.

Across the aisle, in the seat behind Olive Wallace, Jen Cooper was pawing through her handbag. Even inside the bus she looked windblown.

"Where did I put my passport?" she muttered to herself.

Winifred Jenkins, who sat gracefully behind her, never had a problem controlling her hair, scarves, handbags, or any other appendage loose, or attached.

"You're improving," she told Jen crisply. "This is the first time you've lost it today."

Jen made an unintelligible sound.

"Why don't you always keep it in the same place?" Winifred continued. "That way you'll know right where to find it."

Allegra frowned. She was witnessing the scorn of the organized for the disorganized. It had begun when they left Paris and had only gotten worse since leaving Nice.

1

She supposed this sort of thing was bound to happen on a tour as small as this. A group of five women either got on each other's nerves or they jabbered to such an extent that no one saw any of the rich French countryside. They were too busy talking about their families and their jobs, or about the lack of soap in the last hotel bathroom.

That, Allegra supposed, was why Olive had hired Brian Gifford to join them on this tour. Not only was he the only man, not counting the handsome young bus driver who didn't speak English but, as tour director, he had to smooth the ruffled feathers in the bus and keep the local population from being offended at every stop. Brian also felt obliged to pound home a certain amount of information about the places they were visiting and the regions they were driving through.

To Allegra it was all too wonderful and exciting to miss: the exquisitely neat little vegetable patches like the one they were passing now, with occasional rows of flowers as if they'd been thrown in for color; the well-tilled farmland; the lawn-like pastureland complete with cows; and the farm buildings snug about the house, some of the farmyards fastidiously neat, some alive with chickens and geese. Were they searching for worms in the summer rain? Allegra kept hoping she'd see pigs looking for truffles, but perhaps they were too far south.

They were passing a vineyard now—miles of purple grapes as carefully tended as an English hedge. Beyond the rolling green rose the twin turrets of a small chateau.

If it hadn't been for Olive, Allegra wouldn't have been able to see any of this. Who cared if she had been brought along as a combination companion, lady's maid, and porter, with overtones of travel agent? When Olive said she'd pay for the entire trip if Allegra would do all the dirty work, Allegra had jumped at the chance.

She and Olive had known each other since they were ten, and even forty years ago, Olive had been a money-maker. The few nickels and dimes Allegra left home with always found their way into the grubby purse with the finger-bending clasp that was as much a part of Olive as the hands she closed it with. As time passed, the purse had become more sophisticated, but it was always there, always full.

Olive's current purse snapped loudly as she waved a ten-franc note at Allegra.

"Buy me some slides of the Le Puy area when we get to Marseilles," she instructed. "Ask Henry to stop when you see a place that might have them. And be sure there's a picture of the Black Madonna with them."

Allegra lowered her head to hide her displeasure.

No *please*, just an order. This was typical Olive, like calling the French driver *Henry* instead of *Henri*. Why hadn't she thought of those slides while they were in Le Puy? It was next to impossible to find slides of a place once you were out of it. Oh well, Allegra had agreed to do Olive's dirty work, hadn't she? How else would she have been able to afford this extravagant trip? Not from Bob's estate, after the expenses of his long illness and death had been paid; not from Bob Jr., with all the costs of a young family to meet; and certainly not from her own inadequate salary, which wasn't being paid at all while she was on her month's leave. Allegra would consider herself lucky if the museum library didn't fill her part-time secretarial job while she was gone.

It was different for someone like Margot Scott, Allegra thought, her eyes resting on the shoulder-length black hair cascading down the seat in front of her. Margot had quit a good New York editorial job to take this trip, but a girl of twenty-three with Margot's charm and, a Master's degree in the bargain, could pretty nearly pick and choose among jobs.

Jen and Winifred, across the aisle, were more in Allegra's class. Neither woman was yet fifty, as she and Olive were, they were still in their mid-forties. They were both unmarried, both struggling to keep their financial heads above water, and both kowtowing to Olive in different but, to Allegra, equally sickening ways. Jen had been the little girl down the street when Olive and Allegra were going out on their first dates. Even then Jen had known it was to her advantage to flatter Olive, and to this day it was still "poor little me" and "how smart you are, Olive darling." Jen might look and act muddle-headed, but she was an excellent accountant, hired part-time by a team of doctors back home and part-time by the law firm that took care of

Olive's legal needs.

Winifred's approach was to keep pointing out how brilliant Winifred was, a brilliant first cousin to the financial wizard Olive Wallace. A brilliant *successor* perhaps? Or was Allegra being nasty? She didn't know Winifred particularly well. She had come to Cincinnati only two years ago, ostensibly to take over a retiring librarian's job, through Olive's pull no doubt. But her real reason for coming to Cincinnati was to protect her interests as Olive's nearest living relative.

There she was, Allegra told herself, being unkind again. The trouble was, this whole trip seemed to give rise to ungenerous thoughts. Everyone in the bus was either, like Winifred and Margot, related to the rich, arrogant, domineering, sharp-tongued Mrs. Olive Wallace; or childhood friends like her and Jen; or dependents like Brian Gifford and, for the duration of this trip, even the French driver Henri.

They were riding in a bus full of trouble, if you asked Allegra.

She had been asked to do something, but her mind kept swinging back to the bus full of trouble. Would there be more of it, or less, after they picked up Elmer Anderson and his wife in Marseilles? Elmer was another relation—not a first cousin like Winifred but, as far as Allegra knew, the only man left on the family tree.

Why had she put it that way? It made her think of things hanging on a family tree, which made her think of hanging trees and those darn gibbets again. All because of the gibbous moon...

Well, Allegra knew she must earn her trip, and at the moment she had slides to buy.

Chapter Two

The first stop, as Allegra had expected, was fruitless. So were the second and third.

Returning for the third time, she stood on the coach step and gave her umbrella a shake. From that angle, she spotted something on the floor under Olive's seat—perhaps a piece of paper. However, by the time Allegra had propped her umbrella where its drip wouldn't soak one of the shopping bags that were beginning to litter the bus, she had forgotten there was something she was going to pick up. Once seated, she noticed Jen, directly behind Olive, staring across the aisle at Margot. Jen's long hair, hung sideways, her head bent sharply as if she were trying to read something on an item inconveniently placed.

Allegra jumped up. She and Jen bumped heads as both dived for the oblong piece of paper under Olive's seat. Allegra's fingers clamped on one corner, Jen's on another. Together they brought up a sheet torn from a scratch pad. Allegra hardly had time to see that there were names written on the left-hand side and dollar amounts on the right before Olive snatched it away.

"What are you two doing with that?" she demanded hotly. "You've got no business looking at—how'd you get it, anyway?"

"It was on the floor," Allegra explained at the same moment that Jen fluttered, "Don't get upset, Olive darling. We didn't read it. We were picking it up for you."

Exactly like thirty years ago, Allegra thought. Still trying to explain themselves to Olive. Well, they were all big girls now, and Olive could like it or lump it.

Olive was clearly lumping it, demanding again just as hotly, "How did you get it, anyway? It was in my handbag. I saw it only a minute ago."

"Didn't you sneeze a while ago, Olive?" Jen said, still trying to placate her old friend. "Couldn't it have fallen out by accident when you got your handkerchief? I'm positive you sneezed when Allegra got out the third time and the rain blew in."

Trust Jen to make it Allegra's fault. That, too, was like old times.

"It could have come out then, Olive," Winifred interjected calmly.

It wasn't like Winfred to back Jen up; their rivalry for Olive's approval was too intense. Winifred, who didn't usually show emotion, was now looking too innocent to be innocent. She must have been trying as hard as Margot to read, what was on that paper, but hoping that Olive hadn't noticed.

"Well, maybe it did fall out," Olive conceded. "Still, no one's got any business reading it."

Allegra returned to her seat, removing herself from the wrangling and rationalizing still going on. Meaningless only seconds before, the paper had now taken on importance. She tried to remember what she had seen. Too bad she wasn't in the spy business. Spies always memorized pages at a time before they chewed them up and swallowed them or flushed them down the toilet.

The paper had contained a list of names—that much was clear. Your own name always stood out on a page or sounded louder than anyone else's in a conversation. Nothing like that stood out on Olive's list, although Allegra had seen something beginning with "A." The only name she was sure of was Jen's—three clear letters at the foot of the list. But there had been many more than two names on that paper. There must have been ten or twelve—and what did the numbers opposite them mean? Allegra had always been more word-conscious than number-conscious. Her only recollection of the number side of the paper was that the size of the last figure—probably a total; she remembered a line above it—was staggeringly large. On the name side there might have been something beginning with "B." Or was it "E"? Or even "S"? Something curly… a great spy she would have made!

"Allegra! Wake up, Allegra!" Olive's commanding voice got through to her.

"Here's another tobacco store."

"Tobacco?" Still absorbed in her thoughts, Allegra began to grope for her umbrella.

"Tobacco store," Olive repeated. "Get out and look for those slides."

How were the others earning their way? Or were they paying in flattery instead? Brian and Henri had definite jobs to do, but Allegra seemed to be the only errand "boy" among the guests. It was lucky that Brian had been able to rent this small bus. Imagine Olive and her entourage on an American Express tour! Of course, there wouldn't even have been a tour if Olive couldn't have her own bus and her own tour director.

Olive had started the rumors flying when she returned home from her last trip to Europe. Not only did she bring Brian back with her, she took him into her big house on the hill as a sort of resident interior decorator, estate manager, private secretary and, on social occasions, the man of the house. Cincinnati was a conservative city, and Olive would have been the first to criticize if someone else had done what she had. He's a gigolo, the largest group insisted, smirking. He's got something on her, another insisted. A third, the smallest and most charitable, said it was probably nothing more than a smart business arrangement for them both. Allegra belonged to this third group. Olive was too puritanical to take on a gigolo and too cagey to be compromised, but she *was,* a good business woman.

When Allegra returned, damp and unsuccessful, Winifred, who was crisp and neat and dry, produced her usual organized suggestion.

"Why don't you wait for a department store?" she said. "When we were in London I found Stonehenge slides at Selfridge's right away, and Jen told me she'd been hunting all over the city. You could go after we unload at the hotel, while Olive's resting, and you wouldn't have to keep opening the door."

How smart Winifred was, and how concerned she was with Olive's welfare! And how stupid Allegra and Jen were! Allegra rammed her umbrella down so hard it almost stood upright.

"What do we shop for in Marseilles?" Margot asked. "Like sweaters in London and perfume in Paris. What's Marseilles famous for?"

"Bouillabaisse," Allegra said grimly.

Brian was the only one who laughed. He was really quite likable, Allegra thought. It was no wonder Olive was interested in him. Whatever their relationship might be, he must fill an empty place in her life. He was young, but not a kid (middle thirties, she guessed), intelligent, energetic, and good-looking, with sharp blue eyes on a tanned face. One thing the neighbors hadn't thought of was that Olive might be going to adopt him.

Maybe the neighbors hadn't thought of it, but Allegra was willing to bet that Jen and Winifred had, and probably Margot too. An adopted son's interest in Olive's estate would be considerable.

Allegra found it gruesome—this preoccupation with how Olive was going to leave her money, especially while she was alive. To make it worse, she was sure that Olive knew it, and was giving each of them plenty of rope. Don't complete that cliché, Allegra told herself firmly. No more gibbets.

The bus stopped at the top of a hill and Brian turned toward the five women.

"From here you can see the Old Town settled by the Greeks about 600 B.C.," he explained, "and probably by the Phoenicians before them. Too bad it's raining, but you can still see…"

It wasn't the rain that was spoiling this beautiful trip that Allegra had looked forward to with such excitement. Here they'd been driving along Marseilles' famous street, La Canebière, for blocks—and she hadn't even looked out of the window. She mustn't let Olive and her blasted money spoil it for her. After all, it was Olive's blasted money that was paying for it.

"Out that way is the Chateau d'If, where the Count of Monte Cristo…" Brian continued.

"Very interesting," Olive murmured.

She broke into a pause with the tone of one who was thinking, *Very uninteresting.*

"Since it *is* raining, I think it would be well to act on Winifred's suggestion and find our hotel," Olive said. "Besides, it's nearly time to meet Elmer's boat."

"It'll be fun to see one of those big Mediterranean cruise ships," Allegra remarked.

"I'm afraid you'll have to forego the pleasure this time," Olive responded. "I'll need you to massage my back. You know what these bus trips do to it. Brian will pick up Elmer and his wife."

If Allegra had kept her mouth shut, they probably would have all gone to the pier. Or maybe she was imagining that Olive took pleasure in frustrating her, the same as she might be imagining the tension on the bus. Allegra was tired from doing all the dirty work. She couldn't even rest in the hotels until Olive went to sleep. If she'd had any idea what sharing a room with her would entail...

Allegra would have accepted the invitation anyway. She couldn't miss a grand opportunity like this, and there were always sleeping pills if she got too keyed up to sleep.

Allegra found it curious that Olive wouldn't want the privacy of a separate room. Whatever made her decide to put Allegra in the adjacent twin bed, it wasn't to save money. Each of the other guests had a separate room and bath at every hotel they stayed in. Even Brian and Henri had rooms of their own, which was more than generous. Allegra knew what everyone had because she'd made the reservations herself. Maybe poor Olive was actually afraid to be alone; perhaps her heart really was bad, as she sometimes claimed it was, and having Allegra near her gave her comfort. Her husband and parents were dead, she had no brothers and sisters, and she'd never had children. Winifred was a first cousin, but Olive hardly knew her until she moved to Cincinnati. Allegra was, in fact, the oldest friend she had.

The bus drew up to their hotel. Getting out in a warm glow of understanding, Allegra forgot her hostility, and was startled when Brian whispered, "Madame really got to us both this morning, didn't she?"

Allegra laughed. She was amused by the way Brian said *Madame*, with the accent on the second syllable, when he was talking about Olive, and *Olive* to her face. He had a knack for saying the one thing that pleased whomever he was talking with, or entertained them, or maybe even thrilled them, according to who they were. Every woman on the tour had responded to his charm.

As Allegra collected passports and handed out room assignments, she thought back to the beginning of the trip. Both bus and driver had been engaged by mail before the tour started, but neither satisfied Brian after he saw them. While he was trying out substitutes in Paris, Olive had taken Winifred, Jen, and Allegra to London. The four women were noticeably getting on each other's nerves by the time Brian telephoned that the safari was ready to proceed. They had all been delighted with Henri, not only with his driving, but even more with his good looks and good nature. His lack of English had not seemed a drawback until Margot flew in from New York after winding up her job and joined their tour in Nice. Then it seemed a shame that the two attractive young people were unable to communicate—verbally, amended Allegra, as she watched them looking at each other over the heap of luggage in the lobby. Maybe by the time the trip was over Henri would have learned English or Margot French.

Meanwhile, there was Brian, who did speak English and was obviously interested in Margot too. As any man would be, thought Allegra, wondering how anyone with such smooth, tanned skin, such lustrous black hair, and such an attractive, trim figure could possibly be related to Olive.

Handing Winifred a card with her room number on it, Allegra saw Brian move over to Margot's side of the luggage heap and call something in French to Henri, who nodded and walked out the door toward the car. Brian smiled down at Margot, gave her a little spank, and followed Henri outside.

Allegra had been amused at first, but now she was troubled about the way the older women were taking Brian's defection. On the surface, Olive showed little difference. She demanded attention no matter who arrived and seemed to sit back and observe the whole thing as if she had planned it. Maybe she had. But Winifred grew increasingly sharp-tongued and Jen more muddled and forgetful than ever. From Paris to Nice, they had shared Brian's attention. Allegra had watched Olive's self-satisfaction reach almost purring stage under Brian's skillful hands, as well as his words. On several occasions he covered one of Olive's hands with his or gave her a quick squeeze across the shoulders.

Sex, it seemed, always worked.

It worked on Jen and Winifred, too. Jen had come in more than once from a session on the terrace with Brian, her glasses magnifying her well-known starry-eyed look. She had taken to surreptitious hair-combings on the bus, and a generally neater, happier look was beginning to replace the baffled, hopeless look she had developed over the years. She hadn't even lost her passport between Paris and Nice, where Margot joined the tour.

Winifred looked almost human. Sharp-voiced and excessively neat, she had always seemed insensitive to Allegra. But after one of her sessions with Brian these qualities receded, and something that was almost warmth took over. Once or twice, though, Allegra thought she looked worried.

As Allegra tipped the bellboy and closed the door behind Olive's last bag, she chuckled. She'd been having a good deal to think about Olive's and Jen's and Winifred's reaction to Brian. What did they think about hers? Except her sessions with Brian were strictly business. Should she feel neglected? She was certainly better-looking than either Olive or Jen, though she was ten years older than Jen and didn't have Olive's money. Or anyone else's, she thought wryly.

What in the world are you laughing at?" Olive demanded. She was leaning back in the only comfortable chair with her feet up, watching Allegra unlock the suitcases.

"Nothing," Allegra said, although that would never satisfy Olive. "I—I was thinking how hard the so-called language barrier must be to a pretty girl like Margot and a handsome young man like Henri. They're so obviously interested in each other."

"Nonsense," Olive said. "Henry's a mechanic, and Margot'll have money someday."

How had Olive arrived at that conclusion? The job Margot had given up for the sake of this trip was a good one, especially for a young woman, but you would have to have top executive billing to be able to regard a salary as "money." Certainly Margot's father, who had been Olive's first cousin, hadn't been able to leave any money to his widow and daughter. Unless Olive herself... Allegra looked at her curiously.

"Why not?" Olive answered her look. "If she came into most of my estate, or even a substantial part of it..."

11

"Does she know you're considering such a thing?" Allegra asked.

"Why not?" Olive said again. "It'll make her think twice before stepping out of line."

"Quite a whip hand you have there, Olive," Allegra smiled.

"You've got to get something out of money besides responsibility—and possessions," Olive said. She looked down complacently at the large diamonds that blazed on both hands.

Allegra considered the sole small diamond on her left hand. Maybe possessions mattered to some people, but she'd had thirty good years with Bob, happy times and troubled times both. Olive needed those gorgeous rings; she couldn't have had a very satisfying life with her husband Orrin, who may have been the richest man she knew, but certainly wasn't the most generous or the most attractive or the most fun—like Bob.

Olive had taken a long time to make up her mind. Orrin and Bob had come to town about the same time, but Allegra and Bob had been married for almost a year and she was already pregnant with Bob Jr. before Olive married Orrin. Maybe it was the twenty-year difference in age that had made her hesitate, because no one could say that money wasn't important to Olive. It was too bad they hadn't had children. If there'd been any little Wallaces or even one little Wallace, Olive wouldn't be worrying now about Margot "stepping out of line."

By the time Allegra had finished unpacking, a light tap on the door reminded her that answering it was one of her duties.

Brian was waiting in the hall. He looked past her at Olive.

"I've let the Andersons into their room," he said. "You might be interested—" He broke off and glanced at Allegra.

Olive opened her handbag.

"Why don't you look for those slides now, Allegra?" she said. "You can put away the bags when you get back. Here's money for a taxi. The driver will know where to take you."

Not unless he speaks more Anglais than Henri, thought Allegra impatiently. Besides, she, too, was interested in what Brian had to say about the Andersons.

"Ask the concierge where to go, Allegra," Brian called after her.

Brian's instructions were useful, as always. This time Allegra returned with the slides.

Chapter Three

As Allegra came into the lobby, she saw Margot and Jen sitting in the farthest corner, their heads close together. When she approached, Margot stood up, straight and graceful, and walked to the elevator. Jen remained in her chair, staring at the heavily weighted room key in her lap. Her hair was knotted, her glasses were halfway down her nose.

"What is it, Jen?" Allegra asked. "Is there something wrong with your room?"

"I didn't find anything," Jen said. "It's like all French hotel rooms, with one of those funny long bolsters on the bed instead of pillows."

She paused for a moment, pushing her glasses into place.

"Allegra," she burst out suddenly, "have you seen Cicely Anderson, Elmer's wife?"

Allegra shook her head.

"She—she's stunning!" Jen said. "Tall and skinny and svelte—like *Harper's Bazaar.* She looks more French than the French, and she's absolutely gorgeous!"

"What a break!" Allegra laughed. "We could use a little gorgeousness on this tour. Even Margot isn't all that exciting."

"A break?" Jen interrupted. "She makes Margot look like a hick, and the rest of us…"

"That's what I mean." Allegra said. "Up to now you could hardly refer to the Wallace tour as a glamour group."

She sobered abruptly. Jen looked inexplicably miserable. What did it matter if a swan landed in the duck pond? Surely Jen had no idea of competing with anyone, except for Olive's tangible favors. And glamour wouldn't make any difference to Olive, only to a man—Brian! That starry-eyed look behind her hornrims... as far as Allegra knew, there had never been a romance in Jen's life. And now, of all people, Brian.

Poor Jen, Allegra thought.

"She's married, you know," Allegra said. Cold, Victorian comfort, were the only words Allegra could find.

"As if that makes any difference!" Jen said.

Poor Jen, Allegra thought again.

At dinner that night, Jen's words became clear. Cicely was poised, assured, and gorgeous. Wearing a slinky black sequined dress that made her look like a mermaid, with her pale hair coiffed to bring out the purity of her cheekbones, she actually did make Margot look like Miss Cornsilk of 1970, and the three middle-aged women at the table look like—three middle-aged women.

Three? There should be four. Had Jen taken the arrival of the glamorous stranger so hard that she wasn't even going to eat dinner?

Then Allegra saw her stumble through the double doors of the dining room. She was wearing a new, pale blue, young girl dress. Allegra watched her making her way uncertainly among the tables under the glittering crystal chandeliers and muffled an audible, "My God, she can't be drunk!"

Jen bumped into a chair at the small table where Henri sat in a chauffeur's isolation, his back toward his employer and her guests. He started to rise, but Jen kept on coming.

Allegra shot a quick glance around their own table. Had anyone else noticed her erratic progress? Both men, of course, were looking at the mermaid. So was Margot. But Olive and Winifred were staring at Jen. If she was drunk and Olive realized it...

John Calvin was a loose-living libertine compared with Olive. She was mostly uptight about sex, but also felt so strongly about drink that, here in this country of superlative wines, she would not allow wine on her table.

"Why anyone thinks they look better without glasses when they can't see where they're going," Winifred muttered.

Of course—no hornrims. Jen knew that men seldom made passes at girls who wore glasses. On the other hand, you had to be able to grope your way to where the men were.

"Where did you ever get that sweet dress, Jen?" Winifred asked with a sugary-sweet smile. "I looked all over Paris for one like it for my niece. She's only sixteen and would faint with rapture at the idea of a dress from Paris."

"I bought it in Nice," Jen said.

Without glasses, Jen's eyes looked more vague than ever; they were the same wishy-washy blue as her dress. She began to twist her hair nervously.

"You don't think it's too young for me, do you?" she asked. "The woman in the store said..."

No matter how vague she looked, Jen wasn't dumb. Foster McKane, Olive's special lawyer in her firm of lawyers and a friend to all three women, had a high opinion of Jen's ability as an accountant.

"French salesgirls—" Olive began.

Whatever she was about to say wasn't going to be kind.

"It's a beautiful dress," Allegra rushed in warmly. "The French certainly have that touch of something, don't they?"

After dinner, as they were all standing in the lobby, Allegra realized that for the first time she was really looking at Elmer Anderson. The sensation his wife created had overshadowed him, but nothing could overshadow him standing up. He was taller and broader than Brian or any other man in the room. Olive had always referred to Elmer as being "in rubber," which Allegra discovered meant he was a tire salesman, but it was hard to shake off the picture of a middle-aged man with a paunch wearing one of the tight rubber wet-suits skin-divers wear. On the real Elmer, no paunch was visible. He was a good-looking man of about forty, at least fifteen years older than his wife.

Olive tucked her handbag under her arm and began her usual nighttime speech, "I don't know what the rest of you want to do, but my poor tired back needs a rest."

She was startled into silence by Brian's voice.

"Don't you think we ought to see something of the famous night life of

Marseilles?" he said. "You lovely ladies shouldn't be wasted on the desert of your hotel bedrooms."

Olive looked disapproving.

"Count me out of the night life," she said. "My back has all it can take now. And I'll need Allegra."

Brian took his eyes off Cicely long enough to murmur "Cinderella" to Allegra.

"Where's Margot?" he added, glancing around the room.

He called her room without an answer, so they went without her. Elmer gallantly walking between Winifred and Jen, while Brian crooked an elbow at the shining mermaid.

On her way to the elevator with Olive, Allegra spied Margot. They were passing the bar, which had none of the semi-dark privacy of an American cocktail lounge. There was plenty of light to see Margot's long black hair slanted toward the table as she leaned forward, smiling at the young man across from her. Perhaps someone she'd met on the plane from New York...

It was Henri—the best-looking man in the room, with the most charming smile. Wine glasses stood before them both; Margot was evidently making up for a nonalcoholic dinner and crashing the language barrier at the same time.

Allegra turned quickly toward Olive, asking solicitously how her back was holding out and, with a hand on her arm, steered her firmly toward the elevator.

Chapter Four

The rain stopped, so they spent the next day sightseeing. In the bright summer sunlight they walked along the quay in the Old Harbor, exclaiming over the variety of gleaming fish neatly stacked in boxes on stands on the street and on the fishing boats drawn up to the quay. They examined vegetables that looked polished and Henri, who had parked the coach and joined the walking tour, found a flower stand and bought a gardenia, which he presented to Margot with a Gallic flourish. Even Olive could find no objection, although Allegra heard her talking to Brian about Henri not knowing his place, and it being time he returned to the parked car. Brian insisted that Henri was needed to help the ladies over the rough cobblestones and to protect them from the cutthroats of a waterfront well-known for crime. This silenced Olive. She did not see Brian wink at Allegra.

By lunchtime, Henri remained a third man to steady the ladies' steps and to carry an increasing number of packages. He could hardly be turned away from the table, although Allegra witnessed an argument between Olive and Brian before they went out to the sparkling, umbrella-splashed terrace of a restaurant above the Old Harbor.

"Our ship must be in Barcelona now," Cicely wistfully said to Elmer once they were seated. "I did want to see—"

"My, how envious the Pendletons were of our opportunity to see Carcassonne," Elmer said. "When do we go there, Olive?"

Allegra supposed that Elmer was administering a husbandly kick under the table, if you could imagine kicking a mermaid. Without that shimmering dress Cicely no longer looked like a mermaid, but she was no less beautiful in her daytime clothes.

"In a few days," Olive said vaguely. "When are we due in Carcassonne, Allegra?"

Before she could answer, Elmer spoke to Cicely quickly and quietly, as if he were afraid that next time his wife would make it unmistakably clear that she'd rather be on the cruise ship than with Olive's little tour.

"Think of what a wonderful chance we'll have to exercise our French, with Henri speaking nothing but, and Brian speaking French as well as English," Elmer said. "Ask Henri how long it takes to get to Carcassonne from Marseilles. He can't understand what we're saying now, so you can really test your French."

Money was a magnet, thought Allegra. Elmer, too, had no doubt been having fun on the cruise ship, a lot more fun than being stuck with a small group of women under the thumb of a fanatically rigid hostess who objected even to wine with their meals. But this hostess also had hundreds of thousands of dollars, maybe even millions, and no children to leave them to. What else would lure people like the Andersons and Margot and Brian—and maybe even Jen and Winifred—to this group? Was Allegra the only one who had come simply for the trip?

At dinner that night Jen wore another new dress, this one yellow. Not another young girl dress this time, but the color made her look as yellow as the dress. Neither one had been cheap. She must have spent herself poor in Nice, Allegra thought.

"Let's go out on the town again," Elmer suggested, while they were still at the table.

This time Margot and Henri joined the party. Henri looked as much at ease as Margot's escort as he did behind the wheel of the bus. His clothes presented no foreign look. He looked the same as the other two men and was, without question, the most handsome of the three. The touch of deference in his manner was a welcome change after the brashness and even rudeness Allegra had seen too much of in America and England.

As they were all leaving, Olive called, "We're leaving for Nîmes tomorrow morning, so don't stay out too late."

"Our reservations in Nîmes aren't until the day after tomorrow," Allegra said.

"We were going to have another day in Marseilles," Brian added.

"I've changed my mind," Olive said. "Allegra, you'll have to change the reservations."

That settled it, of course; the hostess had changed her mind.

"We can't get seven rooms at the drop of a hat, Olive," Allegra said.

"Then you'd better get on the phone and start trying," Olive snapped.

Several calls to Nîmes revealed no reservations available for the next night at the Imperator, the Cheval Blanc, or the Midi. The Carrière, which was listed in Michelin's *Guide* as having a restaurant and an elevator, had only two rooms free. In a lesser category, the Provence showed an elevator but no restaurant, and had three rooms free.

Allegra put down the receiver.

"We'll have to split up," she announced to the group. "Looks like we'll have to go to three or four different hotels to find enough rooms."

A month ago, not being able to stay at the same hotel would have been catastrophic, and due entirely to Allegra's inefficiency. Now it was just one of those things.

When she finally found two rooms at a third hotel, Olive said, "That'll do, Allegra. It's not as nice as if we could all be together, but the Andersons can chaperon Jen and Winifred. The two men can be in one hotel, and you and I can look after Margot."

Look after Margot? Did Olive think that going to Nîmes a day early would keep Henri away from Margot? All this talk of chaperons may have been Olive's brand of humor, since she was connecting them with Jen and Winifred, but Olive really was living in another generation. Allegra thought that her attitude would be funny if it didn't make everyone so uncomfortable.

The sound of tearing paper brought Allegra's thoughts back to the room she was in. While she had been making her endless string of telephone calls and struggling to make herself understood, Allegra was vaguely aware that Olive had been sitting at the writing table. Now she was tossing scraps of paper into the wastebasket. Olive rose, dusting off her hands as if she had accomplished some not-very-clean but necessary task, and went into the bathroom, locking the door behind her.

Locking the bathroom door might be automatic, but it was one more indication of Olive's desire for privacy. That was what made her wanting to share her room with Allegra so out of character. Tearing up what she had written so Allegra couldn't read it was another example of Olive's—well, secretiveness was what it was.

There were no addressed envelopes lying on the table waiting for stamps. There were no postcards. Of course, Olive might have taken them into the bathroom with her. Postcard messages couldn't be hidden in envelopes. Olive might have written on a postcard or on a dozen postcards—there was plenty of time while the telephoning was in mid-spate—"Allegra Tate is a rat fink." But you didn't tear up postcards.

Allegra had been brought up to respect the privacy of others and certainly not to read their mail or anything they'd written. Allegra had been brought up not to snoop.

It was the rat fink, then, who tiptoed to the wastebasket.

Inside were torn pieces of paper covered with writing. It was clear, distinct writing, Olive's best. Allegra was barely far-sighted enough to read, *To my cousin*—the rest was torn. She looked quickly at the bathroom door. Surely there would be water running before Olive came out, some sort of warning. Even the click of a key...

The rat fink reached for a handful of scraps. Parts of names: *Elmer An—, Jennifer Coop—, Wini—*. The word *dollars* appeared several times. Then, *being of sound and disp—*.

It was a will. Allegra dropped the scraps back into the wastebasket. Olive's will was no business of hers.

Suddenly the sheet of paper that had been under Olive's seat on the bus made sense—the names going into her will and the sums to be given. No wonder Olive had been upset when she thought the others were reading that list. But she shouldn't leave that kind of thing in a wastebasket. Anyone could take the scraps out and piece them together. Allegra could imagine

Winifred and Jen and Elmer with their hands on those scraps. And, yes, even Margot. If she wasn't interested, why had she come on what must seem to her like an old ladies' outing?

At that moment, Allegra was the only person except Olive herself who had access to the torn-up will, but tomorrow morning everyone would be in and out.

The next morning, everyone was. Allegra tried to mount guard over the telltale wastebasket. She had done the packing the night before except for the last-minute things, but she couldn't stay in one spot all the time, especially the spot around the wastebasket. She would draw attention to the wastebasket by hovering.

By ten o'clock, they were ready to leave. With one foot raised toward the bus step, Allegra jerked it back down.

"I forgot—I've got to go back and see—" she said.

She ran into the hotel. She *had* to take one last look at the wastebasket. She had been off guard duty too many times. Someone could have...

And someone had. The scraps of paper were gone.

Chapter Five

Allegra took the elevator down and got into the motor coach. It took real nerve to snatch something out of someone else's wastebasket with the occupants of the room standing around, and others going in and out. There was always a chance that, in preparation for departure, the room might be empty long enough, but what if it wasn't? What if someone came in as you were bending over? You could always drop something of your own into it and say that was what you were picking up.

But you would have to be moved by unbearable curiosity, which was usually, not always correctly, regarded as a feminine characteristic. In the bus, Allegra did a rapid head count. Six women to three men. A man could be as curious about the terms of a will as a woman. But she was getting ahead of herself. How would anyone know that a will was even involved? That sheet of paper under Olive's seat in the bus... who had seen it? She and Jen had both held it in their hands. Margot had gotten a sideways look at it. Maybe Winifred, too, had been able to crane her neck enough to get an idea of what was there. If so, they had all three been smarter than Allegra, who had not connected it with a will until she had seen the scraps in the wastebasket.

But no one really needed to have seen the sheet of paper to know that a will was involved. Allegra considered what Olive had said about Margot being kept in line by the prospect of coming into money. Margot, then, must know about the will. Olive implied that she had told her. Any or all of the people on this bus—except Henri—were people who might logically expect, or at least hope, to inherit something from Olive upon her death. And if she had told Margot, Olive might very well have told the others too. But you

23

didn't inherit until the maker of the will died. This, without admitting it, was what was bothering Allegra. A will could be changed a hundred times while the testator was alive. The testator had to *die* to make it effective.

In the bright sun, inside the warm bus, Allegra shivered.

Chapter Six

L ooking back, Allegra thought of this not as the day they danced under the Pont d'Avignon, or as the day they saw the Pont du Gard, but as the day the accidents began.

They were passing by miles and miles of endless vineyards, and the bus was alive with lively chatter. Allegra tried her best to admire the scenery, but part of her mind kept thinking about Olive's will.

"Will we be going through Arles, Brian?" Elmer asked.

"We're on the road to Avignon right now," Brian said. "We could turn back and go through Arles. What do you want to do, Olive?"

Olive lifted her head.

"We saw Avignon on our way to Nice," Brian continued, "but Margot and the Andersons haven't been there. This road is particularly pretty, and the Pont du Gard is between Avignon and Nîmes. If we see the Gard today, as you suggested, and go through Arles, we'd have to go to Nîmes twice."

"If we keep on this road, will we bypass Avignon?" Margot asked, without waiting for Olive to reply.

"No, the road goes through it," Brian said.

"I'd love to see Avignon and the old bridge the song was written about—the one where people danced and sang," Margot said. "It's still there, isn't it?"

"Well, half of it anyway," Brian said. "It's your decision, Olive."

Brian was determined *not* to ignore their hostess.

"What's at Arles that we'd want to see?" Olive asked.

"More Roman ruins," Brian said. "Similar to the ones at Nîmes. The Colosseum's a little larger in Arles, and there's an old cemetery that's supposed to be something special."

Cicely Anderson gave a girlish squeal.

"Cemetery!" she said. "I vote for the bridge. Dancing and singing are more my style."

"Whatever Olive wants to do, of course," Elmer said primly. Allegra wondered if he was kicking the mermaid again.

"Avignon really is beautiful," Olive said. "It has a wall, too, as well as the river and the Pope's Palace. If you girls want to see it, and we won't be missing much at Arles, I'm sure the rest of us won't mind seeing Avignon again. Besides, we must be halfway there."

"Van Gogh and Gaugin used to live in Arles," Allegra remarked. "We might see that bridge Van Gogh painted, of the woman washing clothes. But, as Olive says, we're halfway to Avignon now, and it certainly bears looking at twice."

For the moment, in the heat of practical discussion, Allegra forgot all about wills and scraps of wills. As the bus rolled toward Avignon, she was once more acutely conscious of her fellow passengers. Perhaps it was her own knowledge of someone's interest in Olive's will that made her imagine an increase in tension in the bus. Perhaps the addition of Elmer and Cicely was responsible. When they had picked Margot up in Nice, the tension had certainly increased. At the time, Allegra had connected it with Brian; after all, from Paris to Nice, there had been only the four older women to claim his attention. The addition of a pretty young girl had noticeably redirected that attention, and Allegra remembered the poorly concealed disappointment of both Jen and Winifred.

Allegra thought back to the days when she and Brian had been arranging the trip.

"Who's coming, Olive?" she had asked.

"Just her nearest and dearest," Brian had answered. "Winifred Jenkins, of course, as her nearest living relative. Margot Scott and Elmer Anderson as the two next nearest, in fact the only others. Anderson's wife has to be included, of course, which won't be any strain as I hear she's quite a dish. To top off the list, you and Jen Cooper, her two oldest friends. To say nothing of yours truly, without whom the trip would be nothing."

"Don't sell yourself short, Brian," Olive had said. "You're an important member of this household."

And he was. Allegra had thought so then, and she thought so now. Whatever their relationship, Brian had certainly made himself indispensable. That was the trouble. There was too much nearest and dearest and indispensable stuff on this bus. Anyone here, as she had told herself earlier, might benefit under Olive's will. Allegra's thoughts went back to the empty wastebasket. The scraps didn't give the terms of the current will, only what they had been, but *someone* was keeping track.

"Next stop, Avignon," Brian announced from the front of the bus.

"There's the wall," Cicely said, pointing.

"Isn't that the old bridge, Brian?" Margot asked. "The one that stops in the middle of the river?"

"The Pont d'Avignon, no less," he confirmed. "Actually, it's the Pont St. Benézét, named for its builder. We'll be there in a minute, and we can all get out. Look at the walls, girls. See how the archers' windows overhang the lower part."

"The better to shoot you with, my dear—twang!" Elmer growled playfully. One arm went forward, the other back as if he held a bow and arrow.

Elmer thought he was being funny, but Allegra began to shiver again.

"Would they pour boiling oil from there, too?" Margot asked.

"I guess so, but this wouldn't be as good as the walls of Carcassonne," Brian told her. "You might be able to crouch under the overhang here and have the oil miss you. But at Carcassonne it would never miss you. That wall's a straight drop."

"I wish you wouldn't keep saying 'you,'" Allegra murmured.

Brian laughed and said something in French to Henri, who pulled off the road and stopped the bus near the bridge.

They all got out and walked to the edge of the bank.

Margot flung out both arms.

"On the bridge of Avignon, everyone passes, everyone dances," she sang. Hair flying backwards, she looked up at the four stone arches reaching into the Rhône. "Come on, everyone, let's dance."

They all began to mill around, laughing and bumping…

Suddenly, a scream, a splash…

"Olive!" Cicely gasped.

Allegra froze. Here it was. It had happened.

Another splash. Henri had dived—a long, forward-going dive, followed by powerful strokes that brought him even with Olive in seconds. To the watchers on the bank, those seconds seemed like hours before they saw him grasp Olive under the arms and start to tow her to shore.

On the bank, near Henri's kicked-off shoes and dropped jacket, Elmer was vigorously brushing off his clothes. Had he fallen?

"What happened?" Allegra cried. "How did—?"

"God knows," Jen said, who was nearest. "Everything seemed to happen at once. I think Elmer fell down—"

"I tripped," he said sheepishly. "I don't know how in hell—"

"He fell flat on his face—"

"And bumped into Olive, right at the edge of the bank."

Everyone was talking at once. They all seemed to have seen more than Allegra, but only a snatch here and a snatch there. No one had seen enough to tell a connected story. The only certainty was that, in the course of the wild gamboling they called a dance, Elmer had fallen and lunged into Olive, who had gone over the bank into the river.

Elmer was still looking for something he could have tripped on while the others were exclaiming over Olive's wet clothes. Henri was wet, too, but only Margot seemed to notice.

"My God, Olive, your handbag!" Allegra exclaimed. "It went in with you."

"How lucky it came out with her!" Winifred said dryly.

"It never would have," Olive said, "if I hadn't had it on the shoulder strap and hung it around my neck. It had everything in it. That's why we have to carry these big handbags. Passport and travelers' checks and French money and toilet paper and heaven knows what. It's going to be hard to dry out. I hope my antacid pills and fountain pen won't be ruined."

"We'll have to get you into dry things, Olive," Allegra said. "You can't travel all the way to Nîmes like this. Why don't we have lunch at the place we stayed on the way to Nice? They must have some room where you can change. Even if Le Prieuré is full up for lunch, I'm sure they'll help us out since we stayed there earlier. Come on. It's just a few minutes across the new bridge to Villeneuve."

Henri, with water trickling from the driver's seat, hurried the bus along the wall, which no one paid any attention to now, across the new bridge, and along the short road to Villeneuve, where he had to slow down on the narrow streets.

The manager of Le Prieuré, tucked away in its once-religious seclusion, listened with horror to Brian's story, placed his own room at Madame's disposal, and offered Henri the facilities of the men's room.

While the others waited, they wandered about the charming hotel, speculating on the ancient building's conversion and salivating over the kitchen aroma.

After lunch, as they drove away from Villeneuve, the old bridge came in sight again, paralleling the new one. Elmer began to hunt again for an explanation of his fall, and to apologize again to Olive for bumping into her. What could he have tripped on that would make him lose his balance so completely?

Allegra was wondering the same thing. A picture of this morning's empty wastebasket flashed into her mind. Now, why had she thought of the wastebasket at this time? Under the Pont d'Avignon, Elmer might have tripped over any number of things, but not over a wastebasket that she had personally left standing in a hotel room in Marseilles. Surely, he couldn't have done it on purpose—or anyone else have tripped him on purpose. Olive was at the very edge of the bank...

But if anyone wanted to make the will effective, Allegra thought morbidly, wouldn't he or she have chosen a time when there was no one around to stage a rescue or arrange some other type of "accident," like a high drop without water underneath? Allegra's eyes went to the city wall, which they were rapidly approaching. She mustn't let Olive climb to the top of that wall or to the walls of Carcassonne, which Brian had said were straight and high. She must also keep Olive from climbing around the Pont du Gard. The pictures she'd seen of it showed a small river below and a lot of rocky ground.

"Do you want to stop at the Popes' Palace, Olive?" Brian asked.

"I think we've seen enough of Avignon," she replied quickly.

"I know I have," Elmer said grimly. "I simply can't think how I could have tripped like that."

Allegra mentally turned off her ears. She'd had enough of Elmer's excuses and apologies, although she also couldn't see how he could have tripped like that. With everybody wildly milling around in their improvised dance, unless you had been looking specifically, watching anyone who got near Olive and anyone who got near anyone who got near Olive, you wouldn't have seen anything. Who had started that crazy dance anyway, a bunch of middle-aged people acting like flower children? Was it Margot? She certainly wasn't middle-aged, and neither were Cicely or Brian or Henri. It was Margot who had suggested coming to Avignon, Cicely who had backed her up, and Brian who had arranged for them to get out at the bridge. But all those moves had seemed natural enough.

What was the matter with her, Allegra thought, impatiently. An accident was an accident. It wasn't on purpose.

It wasn't long before Brian said, "We'll be at the Pont du Gard in a few minutes. There's no need for anyone to get out to see it unless you want to. It's built in three sets of arches. We'll drive across the lowest and there's a place near the road where we can get a good overall view."

Allegra drew a long breath. She was surprised that she was still so tense. Hadn't she just finished telling herself that Olive's accident really was an accident? Now she could enjoy the beauty of the ancient aqueduct without worrying about Olive having another one. There was the small river and the rocky land, and over them stretched, graceful scalloped tiers of stone arches. The enduring work the Romans had left... then the mood was broken by a moving object the Romans hadn't left buzzing across the lowest tier with tourist faces pressed against its windows.

They drew off the road and stopped.

None in their own tour got out. The excitement at Avignon had sobered them all. Allegra missed part of Brian's comments.

"... built by the Romans about the time of the birth of Christ to bring water to Nîmes. The water came in on the very top, above the row of little arches," he said.

"What were the rest of the arches for?" Margot asked.

"Support, and I suppose the lowest row was used for a bridge," Brian explained. "They had to have some way of crossing the river."

"Has everybody seen enough?" Olive asked impatiently. "Then let's get on to Nîmes. Allegra told you, didn't she, that we'll have to split up? She and I and Margot will stay at the Carrière, Elmer and Cicely and Winifred and Jen at the Provence, and Brian and Henry at the Univers. It's too bad, but none of the hotels could make that many rooms available without advance notice. Don't forget, you'll have to let them have your passports. Allegra usually takes care of those things, but we'll be getting off at the first stop, and I'm going to need her, right away."

"Where did I put my passport?" Jen said, scrabbling through her handbag in her usual panic.

Winifred laughed.

"Now I know we're back to normal," she said. "Jen's lost her passport again."

At the Carrière, Olive gave parting instructions to meet there at eight for dinner, and she and Allegra and Margot went up to their rooms. A bang of a nearby door told Allegra that Margot hadn't stayed long.

Olive must have heard it too.

"Don't bother doing a lot of unpacking, Allegra," she instructed. "We'll only be here one night and then we'll all go to the Imperator, where we have our regular reservations. There's something I think you ought to know, in view of that dunking at Avignon."

Olive paused and walked stiffly to a window overlooking the side street.

"We're by ourselves now," she continued. "We've got the end room and Margot's gone out. Though I must say, these old European hotels have thicker walls than the ones at home. I don't suppose anyone could hear unless we were shouting, or someone was listening at the door."

She left the window and walked quickly to the door, opened it, peered out, shut it, and returned to Allegra, who was still standing with one hand on Olive's suitcase on a rack by the closet door, standing with her mouth open.

"I have a feeling, Allegra, that what happened in Avignon was no accident," Olive said. "Have you considered that?"

Olive waited impatiently for an answer.

"The-the thought did cross my mind," Allegra stammered. "But surely you don't think...?"

It was her turn to pause.

"Elmer could have pushed me deliberately," Olive said.

"It's not fair to blame Elmer, Olive," Allegra said. "Something—or someone—really could have tripped him. He keeps insisting he tripped. With all that gyrating around—"

"That's not impossible, of course," Olive said skeptically. "But if he didn't do it deliberately, someone else might have. We don't know for sure, but it *could* have been deliberate."

Allegra nodded thoughtfully. She and Olive were following the same reasoning, but suspicion had always been part of Olive's makeup, not of Allegra's.

Olive was standing by the writing table now.

"Has it occurred to you to wonder why I asked you to share a room with me on this trip?" she said.

Why was she changing the subject? Allegra thought.

"Well, yes, it has," Allegra said. "I've always thought of you as someone who liked her privacy. I thought maybe the packing and unpacking were hard on your back or maybe your heart was acting up..."

That, she thought, was as good a way as any of saying secretive.

"I have a good reason for wanting you with me, Allegra," Olive insisted, "and not just wanting someone with me, wanting *you*. Because I can trust you."

"I should hope so, but—" Allegra said.

"Who else can I really be sure of in this—this pack of wolves?" Olive said. "You're the only one who doesn't have her hand out. You're the only one who isn't waiting for me to die."

"Olive!"

"Don't expect anything from me, Allegra," Olive said sternly.

"Expect anything?" Allegra said. "What do you mean?"

"Don't expect me to leave you anything in my will," Olive said.

"Why should I—you have no obligation to me," Allegra said.

"That doesn't prevent Jen from having her hand out—and Brian," Olive pointed out. "For that matter, none of the others are close enough relatives so there's any obligation on my part. But they're all sitting back on their haunches, drooling."

"But Olive—" Allegra said.

"I have no obligation, and I have no children either," Olive said. "What's more logical than for me to leave my money to the only relatives I have? And they're all with me, all three of them, right here on this trip. I tell you, Allegra, I'm afraid."

Chapter Seven

"But you have years to go, Olive, before you leave your money to anyone," Allegra said. "You're only fifty-three. You could change your will a hundred times before—"

"Not if someone took it into his head to make the current will final," Olive said. "That's what I thought someone had done today when I saw that water rising up to meet me."

"But how would they know what your will says?" Allegra asked. "No one but you and your lawyer—"

Olive made a sound that might have been called a laugh.

"It never occurred to me that anyone would try anything when we were all together, like this morning," she said. "I thought, with you in the room with me at night—"

She paused and began again.

"How would they know? A few days ago, I said you had to get some fun out of having money. Remember? Margot wasn't the only one I told—like a fool. It seemed like fun to let people know I was planning to leave them something substantial—plans that could be changed if they didn't live up to my expectations."

"Olive, how could you?" Allegra said. "How did you—dare to?"

"Living dangerously, I guess," Olive said. "There aren't too many ways for a fifty-three-year-old woman to live dangerously."

"There's always reckless driving," Allegra chuckled. "It might be safer, at any rate. Well, between Brian and me, we ought to be able to protect you. And we can add Henri to that list. He jumped in after you this morning."

"I don't know about Brian, Allegra," Olive admitted. "I told him that if what he claimed was true, he could expect to be named in my will too."

Allegra groaned.

"That leaves only Henri and me, and Henri doesn't speak English," she said. "Of course, there's Jen, but she's so scatterbrained she'd probably be more of a hindrance than a help."

"Count Jen out, Allegra," Olive said confidently. "I've known her so long—like you—but she's such a helpless muddle-head that I..."

"That you told her you'd remember her in your will," Allegra said. "Oh, Olive, can't you see what you've done by all this talking?"

"I can now," Olive said. "And I also see what I'm going to do this minute. I'm going to sit down and make a *new* will and leave Elmer Anderson out of it."

"Because you think he pushed you into the river this morning?" Allegra asked.

"I don't think it; I know it," Olive said.

"His may have been the hand," Allegra said. "But if someone tripped him—"

"It'll teach him to be more careful," Olive said.

"He may never know you've cut him out," Allegra said.

"I'll see that he does," Olive said.

"My God, Olive, haven't you gotten yourself into enough trouble with all this—blabbing you've done about your will?" Allegra said.

"A will can always be changed," Olive said. "You know that, and the others know it too. I've reminded them often enough. Will you get me the yellow tablet that's in the bottom of my big suitcase? Open up my handbag and spread the stuff around to dry."

Back to normal. Olive was issuing orders again.

As Allegra handed her the tablet, someone knocked on the door. She crossed the room to open it.

Brian's attractive smile, momentarily turned on Allegra and then flashed to Olive.

"Everyone's settled in their hotels, and I thought I'd see how you were doing, Olive," Brian said. "Any the worse for this morning's excitement?"

"Why don't you go out and explore the town, Allegra," Olive suggested. "You might pick up some literature on the things to see in Nîmes."

"Right now?" Allegra said. "I haven't unpacked."

"You can unpack later," Olive said. "I want to discuss a few arrangements with Brian. Isn't there something you can find out about the Maison Carrée?"

"I hope you know what you're doing," Allegra muttered as she closed the door. "If any of them want you dead—"

Allegra didn't complete the thought. How could you protect someone who wouldn't cooperate? Especially if that someone was an adult as old as you were and practically your employer. Olive had just finished telling her she was afraid of everyone named in her will. So here she was, alone with the strongest, a man she knew far too little about. What was it Olive had said about a claim? If what Brian claimed was true...

At the time she said it, Allegra had been too bogged down in worry to notice any remark that wasn't directly connected with protecting Olive from her various power grabs. Because that was what telling each prospective legatee about a prospective legacy amounted to, with the threat of changing her will always present. Did power over this handful of people mean more to her than her life? Or was Allegra simply being dramatic again?

What claim could Brian possibly have on Olive—a man she had never heard of until she met him in England two years ago on a summer's tour of Great Britain? A claim that would rate a legacy under her will...

Allegra came to a full stop in the middle of the sidewalk, barely missing a bump from the loaded basket of a fat farm woman in black hurrying along behind her. The woman swerved, and Allegra saw coarse green celery tops, feathery green carrot tops, a long loaf of bread, and a chicken's head on a lolling neck go by. She was letting Nîmes go by, too: the tree-lined streets, the old buildings, the people on the sidewalks—small-town bourgeois, tourists, blue-collar workers, farm men and women, darting children—the drowsy, sun-warmed feeling of the air. For the first time since morning, when she had found the torn-up will scraps were gone, Allegra relaxed.

A window with tourist folders in it brought her back to the problem-filled present. If she picked up the folders now and went back to the hotel, would

Olive be through with her conference?

Brian Gifford... Allegra had never thought about his name before; it was simply Brian's name. Now she thought about the name itself. It had a fancy ring, like a stage name. So did his English accent. Both might be genuine but suppose he had given himself a name and accent to fit some kind of claim he was making on Olive.

Allegra began to walk faster... faster...

By the time she reached the hotel, she was almost running.

The room door was opened by Brian himself, whose attractive smile now looked phony too. All con men had attractive smiles, attractive ways.

"See you both at dinner," Brian murmured in a tryst-making tone as he walked down the hall—striding in a manly way that might be as phony as the rest of him.

Allegra slammed the door.

"Olive, how do you dare to be alone with him?" she demanded. "Once you've told him you're going to leave him something in your will, he's as dangerous to you as any of them. What did you mean by saying if he can make his claim stick? What do you know about Brian Gifford anyway?"

"Don't get so excited," Olive said. "It so happens that I'm not afraid of Brian. Do you think I'd have taken him into my home and given him the management of my property if I was afraid of him?"

"That's the trouble," Allegra said. "That's the way con men work. They get widows to turn over their businesses to them. And pretty soon they get so dependent on them that—"

"Brian's no con man," Olive said. "And I'm still *compos mentis*. He only does what I tell him to. I get his advice sometimes, but I don't have to follow it unless I want to. He saves me a lot of bother and he's a pleasure to have around the house."

"I'm sure he is," Allegra said. "They always ingratiate themselves with their victims."

"I'm no victim," Olive insisted.

"If I were you, I'd be a lot more afraid of Brian than any of the others," Allegra said. "Winifred and Margot and Elmer are your cousins; you know

37

all about their backgrounds. And you've known Jen all her life. But what do you know about Brian?"

"I knew more about him when I took him in than I do about Elmer's wife now, and I know him even better after two years of living in the same house with him," Olive said.

She plunked herself in the chair at the writing table and turned back the top of the yellow tablet.

"Olive, do you know anything at all about Brian except that he drove a car to take a private group sightseeing in England?" Allegra asked.

"The British tourist organization looks into the people who take out tourists, believe me," Olive said. "They have to be responsible, or they don't get the chance. Besides, Brian told me—"

She broke off.

"Told you what?" Allegra asked.

"Well, it's really none of your business, but since you're so upset, I'll tell you," Olive said. "Orrin's people came from England, you know. And Brian claims to be a relative—his cousin's nephew."

So that was what had led Olive to bring him home with her! That was a connection none of the neighbors had guessed.

"But that sort of thing can be proved," Allegra said. "The English keep extremely accurate records. Didn't you have it checked?"

"Of course I did," Olive said. "Unfortunately, the small town where he was born was bombed and all the records burned up."

"What about tombstones?" Allegra said. "They don't burn."

"Brian's parents came from another area, and they were both killed in the London bombings," Olive said. "He was too young when they were alive to care about his beginnings or remember anything about places or relatives."

"That kind of story's a little too convenient for anyone who wants to hide his past," Allegra said. "I suppose he was brought up in an orphanage after his parents died?"

"As a matter of fact, he was," Olive conceded.

"That's too much," Allegra sighed. "Can't you see what a perfect cover-up that kind of story is?"

"Well, it could be," Olive admitted grudgingly. "On the other hand, it could be true."

"It's possible, of course," Allegra said. "But it seems highly unlikely. There are too many coincidences. If you're leaving him money on the strength of a *possible* relationship to your husband, forget it. If you're leaving it to him because he's an attractive young man and you like him, that's another matter. In either event, if you're in any danger from the people who know they're down in your will, you're in exactly the same danger from him that you are from the others. Maybe more so, because how do you know that part of the time he says was spent in an orphanage wasn't spent in prison? Maybe he's a murderer."

"Maybe he is," Olive said dryly. "I've heard some murderers were quite likable people."

"Oh, Olive, don't be ridiculous," Allegra said.

"I'm not being any more ridiculous than you are," Olive snapped. "Now stop bothering me—I want to get this will written."

The will leaving Elmer out. What a situation! Here were all the people named in the will of a wealthy woman (except maybe for a few faithful retainers and charities) living in daily close contact with that woman while she played now-you-see-it, now-you-don't with their names in her will. No wonder Olive was afraid.

Chapter Eight

Dinner brought them all together again. Allegra watched the Andersons to see whether word of their vanished prospects had reached them yet. Except for more than usual solicitude for Olive on Elmer's part, they did as much laughing and talking as on the previous two nights.

The next morning, however, when they assembled for the day's sightseeing, there was a noticeable difference. Elmer looked as if he were on his way to a funeral and Cicely was maneuvering her long-handled umbrella like a weapon. Allegra heard her complaining to Margot, jabbing viciously at the ground around a tree planted at the edge of the sidewalk.

"God, I wish we'd stayed on that ship," she said. "Such a great bunch of people on board, real swingers…"

Margot laughed. "We're a little short of swingers on this tour."

"There was always something fun to do and people who were fun to do it with," Cicely said.

"Forget it, honey," Elmer muttered. "No use making things worse. Maybe we'll have a chance to get in good again if we don't."

Hope dies hard, thought Allegra, but maybe Elmer was right. This was the second time, to her knowledge, that Olive had changed her will. And there had no doubt been plenty of other times. Maybe Elmer would somehow make up for his blunder, and the pendulum would swing back. At least no one had been able to piece together yesterday's will scraps. Allegra had seen to that by burning them after Olive went to sleep. For once she'd been able to put her wakefulness to good use instead of writing postcards and keeping her tour journal up to date. After the last scrap had become ash, she took a sleeping pill.

Before they began their sightseeing, Brian and Henri unloaded their bags at the hotel where their reservations had been made three months ago. Then they started on the rounds of Nîmes, beginning with the Tour Magne, which was indeed a big tower on a hill at the edge of town, going on to the exquisite Roman temple called the Maison Carrée; the Temple of Diana; the Roman baths; assorted Roman gates.

"I thought we'd make the Arena the last stop before lunch," Brian said. "There's a lot to see there, and we'll want time to compare it with the Colosseum in Rome. This one's actually older. Then in the afternoon we can visit the museums."

But they did not visit the museums or even finish comparing Colosseums, because in the Nîmes Colosseum Olive had her second accident.

They all took a look at the dimly lit passageways leading under the Arena; everybody except Margot and Henri turned toward the stairs going up to the spectator seats and the sunshine.

"Don't you wish you hadn't brought that long-handled umbrella, Cicely?" Jen asked, looking down complacently at her own short, folding umbrella. "The sun came out after all, and it's so much easier to carry these. I think they're the only thing for travelers."

"I told her the storm was breaking," Winifred said. She had to be right even about the weather.

Cicely ignored the interruption and addressed Jen.

"Only if convenience means more to you than style," she said coldly. "The long ones are infinitely smarter."

Jen flushed and muttered to Allegra, "I hope she falls over it."

But it wasn't Cicely who fell.

They were standing at the top of the stairs, looking down on the floor of the Arena. Brian, borrowing Jen's folded umbrella, began to demonstrate gladiatorial techniques with the short sword.

Cicely pointed her long-handled umbrella at Brian.

"Suppose someone in the ring had a long sword," she said. "What chance would the men with the short ones have?"

"She wants to prove that long-handled umbrellas were superior even two thousand years ago," Winifred said.

Allegra laughed. It was funny to see how Winifred had stopped picking on Jen as soon as Cicely showed up. She and Jen had banded together against the threatening newcomer.

Spurred on by Winifred's comment, Cicely brandished her umbrella and gave a wild lunge. Brian parried with the short umbrella, and they were off—thrusting, dodging, jumping back and forth on the landing at the head of the steps. The audience had to dodge and jump too or be bumped.

Over the excited squeals and cries of "Look out!" a real scream rose, a scream of terror.

Olive had jumped too far over the edge of the step. She was falling...

Brian dropped his weapon and dashed for the stairs.

Olive plunged down them, head first. But not as fast as Brian ran. He caught her before she was halfway down.

The others began streaming down. By the time Olive had been turned about enough to sit on one of the steps, they were all around her.

"Are you all right, Olive?"

"Whatever happened?"

"Are you hurt?"

"When I looked up, there you were, toppling..."

"Did you turn your ankle?"

"Is anything broken?"

That was what Allegra and Brian were trying to find out, arm by arm and leg by leg.

"Olive, you never cease to amaze me," Brian said. "I can't find anything except a scraped arm. There's nothing broken, I'm sure. But you'll be awfully sore and bruised."

"Thank God you're tough, Olive," Allegra said.

"Let's see how well you can stand," Brian suggested.

With Brian on one side and Elmer on the other, they brought Olive upright, protesting at the pain in her arms. Once on her feet, that pain was forgotten for the pain in one ankle.

"I guess you've wrenched it," Brian said. "And I think you ought to see a doctor. I don't think there's anything broken, but who am I to say? I'm sure the concierge can give us the name of someone who speaks English. If not, I'll be your interpreter."

The doctor confirmed Brian's diagnosis of no broken bones and gave Olive some salve for her scraped arm, some lotion for her sore muscles, a binding on her wrenched ankle, and a sedative for her shaken psyche.

There was no new will that night. The sedative would see to that. But probably, thought Allegra, there would be no one else to cut out anyway. It had been Cicely's umbrella that caused the accident, and the Andersons were already in the doghouse.

Surely this had been a genuine accident. The gladiator act had been, or at least seemed to be, spur-of-the-moment. Brian had started it, but he certainly had not invited anyone else in. Unless he and Cicely had planned the whole thing beforehand. Though if there'd been any advance planning, it would have been between Cicely and her husband, not an outsider like Brian. Winifred's crack about long-handled umbrellas may have brought on the crazy duel, but she could hardly count on it, supposing she had wanted to encourage the wild confusion that led to Olive's accident. No, Allegra told herself firmly, this time it really was an accident. And probably the other one was too.

But when Brian suggested she take a hand in the bridge foursome Jen and Winifred were getting up after dinner, Allegra said she wanted to finish a book. She felt uneasy. She had left Olive to join the others for dinner, but they were all at the table. Things would be different after, with everyone except the card players free to wander about at will. Though what difference that would make since the fall in the Colosseum had been an accident, and the fall into the river had too...

She was being firm again.

"Do you think we'll be able to go on to Carcassonne tomorrow?" she asked Brian.

"I certainly hope so, after the trouble you had getting rooms in Nîmes for one extra night," Brian said. "It's not a long trip. If Olive can walk at all, the motion of the bus will keep her from getting too stiff."

Fortunately, Olive could walk the next morning and was all for going on. She said she'd had enough of the old Roman part of France and was ready to try the Middle Ages.

Tonight, they would be at Carcassonne. The walls of Carcassonne, Brian had told them when they were looking at the walls of Avignon, dropped off high and straight. Why couldn't Allegra get that out of her mind? She was supposed to see the beauty of the old walls, not their danger. But she would make sure, if it was the last thing she did, that Olive didn't do any jumping around on top of those walls; she wouldn't even walk on them if Allegra could prevent her.

They had lunch at Beziers, the only stop they made between Nîmes and Carcassonne.

The coach passengers were unusually quiet. Even Cicely and Margot seemed subdued. Or was it thoughtful? Were they all speculating, as Allegra was, about the two accidents? Either one of them could have been serious, even fatal. Olive was lucky that, on each occasion, an alert young man had seen her in time. Perhaps some of the silent passengers were thinking about what they would have gained under Olive's will if one of the accidents *had* been fatal. But the distance between speculation and action was great, or at least could be great. Allegra was no mind reader, thank God. She wouldn't want to know if one of her fellow passengers was debating whether it was possible that their maneuvering to cause the accidents had been discovered.

Allegra was so deep in disturbing thought that Brian's announcement, "There's Carcassonne!" startled her. Standing on a rise of ground, enclosed within its turreted walls, Carcassonne was a dream city, each rounded tower roofed with a cone of slate.

The dam of silence burst.

"It's unbelievable!" Winifred cried, the first to recover coherent speech.

"It's a mirage," Elmer said.

"Rapunzel might have let down her hair from one of those pointed towers," Allegra said.

"It's like the pictures in Grimm," Jen said.

"Wow! It really is beautiful," Cicely agreed.

"Terrific!" Margot cried.

"*Oo la la,*" Henri said.

With every passing minute, the mirage grew larger but no more real. Soon the new town came in sight on lower ground across the river, and it wasn't long before they were driving through the clutter of low buildings at the foot of the hill leading up to the ancient ramparts. The bus stopped directly below them.

"Look, there's a real drawbridge!" Margot cried. "It looks like it still lifts."

"The moat has water in it," Elmer said. "They're usually bone dry if not half-filled with dirt."

"What are we waiting for?" Olive asked. "Can't we drive in?"

"Take a look," Brian said. "On the other side of the drawbridge."

"I don't believe it," Allegra cried. "A traffic light!"

For once, the tension in the bus turned to laughter.

One at a time, five cars rumbled across the drawbridge. Then the green light came on.

The bus was halfway across when Jen said nervously, "Aren't we too wide to make it?"

"That's what you'll think when we're inside, too," Brian told her. "The streets are almost as narrow as the bridge."

Pedestrians flattened themselves against shop doorways as the coach passed. When it finally reached an open space too small to be called a square, everyone inside drew a deep breath. The next street, only a block long, was wider, with another open space at the end before they dived into a narrow slit of a street made to seem narrower by walls on each side. They came out into a large opening, a real square at last, in front of a cathedral with their hotel at the side of the square.

"Thank God this hotel has a restaurant," Olive said with a loud sigh. "It says so in Michelin, doesn't it, Allegra? I'd hate to walk far on these cobblestones."

As soon as the door had closed behind the last bellboy with the last bag, Olive turned to Allegra.

"See if you can get our rooms here for a couple more days, will you?" she said. "I'm expecting a cable and they may not be able to get the information I want in the time we reserved—five nights, isn't it?"

Allegra nodded, appalled at the prospect of trying to change reservations again.

"By the way, Allegra, don't mention this change to the others yet," Olive said. "When you have to, lay it on my ankle. Say I feel I need more rest. Something like that."

"What about the trips we were going to make from Carcassonne, the ones to Andorra and Narbonne Beach?" Allegra asked. "They won't be restful. Shall I tell Brian to forget them?"

"No, the others can go," Olive said. "They'll have to do something while we're here. I'll have those two days in peace."

Allegra started for the door.

"Don't go to the desk," Olive instructed. "Someone's bound to hear you. Telephone them."

For once Allegra was lucky. A cancellation for a party of four had been received, and the reservations clerk assured her there would therefore be no question of his holding all the rooms for two more days.

"*Enchanté, Madame*," he said.

Allegra was not so enchanted. She found herself ticking off her problems aloud.

"Now I've got to change our reservations at Lourdes and Pau and Biarritz, and maybe even Bordeaux and Les Eyzies," she lamented, "or we have to cancel something somewhere. Oh, God!"

She clutched her head in both hands.

"Nonsense, Allegra, we'll cancel Lourdes," Olive said. "We can see enough by driving around and getting out and walking in a few places. I never did like the idea of sleeping where all those sick people have been. It's probably terribly unsanitary. And we can cut out Pau. All we were staying there for was the view of the Pyrenees, and we can see that driving through. Now you've got your two days."

Olive would make a good business-woman, Allegra thought. She didn't panic and, though she pretended not to know anything about their itinerary, whenever anything came up, she knew as much about it as Allegra and could put her finger right on the easiest spots to change. Of course, if Allegra had suggested those changes, Olive would have wanted something else.

The two cancellations were easy. After her nerve-racking experience calling the Nîmes hotels from Marseilles, Brian had told Allegra to ask the concierge to make the calls for her. By getting him to translate her needs into French, there was no danger of misunderstanding. She made the request by telephone, and before she had finished unpacking the concierge called to report that the cancellations had been made.

As she was hanging the last dress in the closet Olive, sitting at the writing table, held out an envelope.

"There must be a post office in this anachronism of a town," she said. "Will you find it and send this air mail? Don't leave it at the desk downstairs."

Allegra reached for her bag.

"If the only post office is in the new town, get Henri to run you over," Olive added.

"If I can find someone to ask him," Allegra said after she'd closed the door. She was talking to herself pretty freely these days.

In the long hall with its row of benches and straight chairs, she saw Cicely sitting alone. She must be waiting for Elmer, or maybe it was Brian she was waiting for.

She got up and walked toward Allegra.

"You're going out, aren't you?" Cicely said. "Do you mind if I tag along? I haven't seen the town yet."

"Join me if you'd like, but I'm not really sightseeing," Allegra said. "I'm looking for the post office."

"You can leave your postcards with the concierge," Cicely said. "He'll stamp them for you. They always do."

"Olive wants her mail taken to the post office," Allegra said. She didn't have to tell Cicely it wasn't postcards; she had seen the name and address of Olive's lawyer on the envelope. "But I'll have to stop at the desk to find out where the post office is."

They passed the motor coach, which had been moved close to one of the walls that formed the square in front of the cathedral, and started out through the narrow street of walls they had driven through coming in. It seemed to be the only street leading out of the square.

"Oh, look at the groovy postcards!" Cicely said. Postcards seemed to be Cicely's main topic of conversation this afternoon. "I'm going to buy them here to send to all my friends. Carcassonne's the most different-looking place I've ever seen."

Carcassonne certainly was a different-looking place, Allegra thought. She ought to send some cards herself, though it was the small, incredibly old stone shop that caught her attention rather than the colored reproductions of the walled city.

Having exhausted the subject of postcards, Cicely walked beside her saying nothing. Allegra supposed it was because she was much older than Cicely, practically a stranger, and not a man. It was up to Allegra to keep the conversation going.

"The concierge said the post office is across the street from the other hotel, the Donjon," Allegra said. Her needle was stuck on post offices as firmly as Cicely's was on postcards. "I wonder if that's where the dungeon of the old castle used to be."

"What's the name of our hotel?" Cicely asked. Maybe she didn't know what a dungeon was or didn't care. For all Allegra knew, it might have had a different meaning in the Middle Ages anyway.

"The Cité," Allegra answered. "That's what the local residents call this place too, the old walled city."

Cicely said nothing.

They passed a break in the wall that held a terrace restaurant, blooming with blue umbrellas.

"That's attractive, isn't it?" Allegra remarked.

Cicely made no objection to that statement, nor did she indicate agreement. She continued to say nothing.

They were walking between sheer walls again when she suddenly stopped and burst out, "Did you know that Brian is selling information about Olive's will?"

Chapter Nine

Wha—what do you mean 'selling information?'" Allegra stammered.

"You know how Olive keeps changing her will?" Cicely asked. "Every time she gets mad at someone, she makes a new will and leaves them out."

For a newcomer, Cicely certainly was well informed.

"I don't know how Brian finds out, but he always seems to know who's in and who's out and offers to sell that information to anyone who's interested—for twenty-five dollars," Cicely added.

"Does—does he have many takers at that price?" Allegra asked.

"Just about everybody, I guess," Cicely answered gloomily. "Everyone wants to know whether they're still in the will or not."

"Does he know the amount each one's down for?" Allegra asked.

Cicely shook her head.

"I'm not sure he knows that" she said. "Although I suppose he'd sell that information if he had it. Maybe for another twenty-five."

"That could get expensive," Allegra murmured, still stunned.

"I thought I'd mention it," Cicely said. "I don't suppose he's approached you, with you being so close to Olive. Well, I guess I'll go back and pick up those postcards. See you later."

Allegra stood there staring after Cicely, whose shapely hips swung with each step down the narrow, walled street. Olive had called Carcassonne an anachronism, but maybe *they* were the anachronisms—the tourists filling the cobbled streets with their drip-dry dresses and no-press slacks, filling the air with loud talk in languages strange to these walls—American English and English English, German, Italian. Most of the tourists were loud talkers. They weren't like Cicely, who had imparted her confidential news in private.

But Allegra couldn't distract herself with philosophical comparisons between the inhabitants of the Cité in the centuries before Columbus was born and the people who walked the streets now. She had a decision to make. Should she tell Olive what Brian was doing? Olive had more than enough worries now, but shouldn't she know that Brian was passing along everything he learned about her will, so she could watch what she said?

If Brian was the one who had robbed her wastebasket… but the information those scraps contained, once pieced together, would be out of date. The up-to-date information must come from the horse's mouth.

Allegra was still undecided at dinnertime. Then, as they rose from the table, she made up her mind. She heard Olive tell Brian she wanted to talk with him. Allegra must get there first, to warn her.

But she didn't. Jen detained her with a question about the next day's activities and by the time Allegra reached her room, Brian had unlocked the door and was returning the key to Olive, with one hand on the doorknob.

"Later, Allegra," Olive said firmly. "I have some things to go over with Brian."

Like wills? What would Brian have to sell as a result of this conversation? Allegra walked in angry pounces up and down the hall. Winifred came up and went to her room, Jen went to hers, and Allegra kept walking.

At last Brian came out. He grinned at Allegra.

"Your turn," he said smugly. "Madame is ready."

For once she didn't respond. She glared at him and closed the door so hard it slammed.

"Olive, do you know what that man's doing?" Allegra said. She was wasting no time now.

"Brian?"

"Yes, Brian, your fair-haired wonder," Allegra said. "He's selling information about your will!"

"He's doing what?" Olive asked.

"Selling—every time you change your will, he goes to the people you've named in it—the people on this tour—and offers to give them the latest dope—for a price," Allegra said.

A peculiar expression that might have been a smile twitched Olive's face. "What kind of price?" she asked.

"A dollars and cents price, what else?" Allegra said. "He's the biggest money-grabber of them all."

"Perhaps you overestimate Brian," Olive said. "Or the others are bigger money-grabbers than you think. How much does Brian make on these transactions? What's his going rate?"

"Twenty-five dollars," Allegra said.

"You mean each time I change my will, he offers to tell what the change is for twenty-five dollars?" Olive asked.

"So I'm told," Allegra said. "If that isn't the dirtiest—"

"He gets twenty-five dollars from each person he tells?" Olive asked. Her peculiar expression had turned into a full-fledged smile.

"Yes."

Olive's smile burgeoned into a laugh.

"At the rate I've been making changes, that should be quite a money-making enterprise," Allegra said. "I didn't know Brian had it in him."

"There are lots of things you don't know about Brian," Allegra said.

"So you've said before," Olive said. "How did you pick up this tidbit? Did he try to sell to *you*?"

"Cicely told me," Allegra said.

"The Andersons' bad news still rankles, naturally," Olive said. "You don't drop a hundred thousand dollars like gum wrappers. That ought to make them think twice about the way they fling around their arms and their umbrellas."

"A hundred thou—Olive!" Allegra said. "Did Brian know how much was involved?"

"I talked it over with him a year ago, and several times since," Olive said.

"Olive Wallace, how you can—" Allegra said.

"I know. I know," Olive said. "I was a fool for talking to any of them, including Brian. If instead I'd hinted that I might leave them something, I'd probably have gotten what I wanted out of them without being afraid for my life. And I thought it was fun to live dangerously!"

"Well, it's too late now; the damage is done," Allegra said. "Besides, if Brian knew who you were leaving money to and how much, and all the changes you made, word would have gotten around anyway."

Olive made a game attempt to laugh.

"Maybe he started selling information before we left on our trip," she said.

"Your lawyer's the only one you should be discussing the terms of your will with," Allegra said.

"Don't rub it in," Olive said. "I must say, I'm glad I brought you along. Not that you can undo anything I've done, but it's good to know I've got someone around I can count on."

She stood up.

"Will you unzip me, Allegra?" she continued. "It's early, I know, but I find I'm astonishingly tired, and my ankle hurts. I think I'll go to bed."

She was hardly in bed before she fell asleep.

Chapter Ten

Allegra was too keyed up to read. Locking her sleeping roommate inside, she picked up her handbag and hurried outside into the pleasantly warm, faintly star-lit night. In this section of the old city the streetlights were strong enough only to dim the stars, but as she scuffed along the cobblestones toward where the small stores were clustered—and where cars waited for the traffic light to let them go through the narrow main street to the drawbridge—the lights were brighter, and the stars were almost lost.

She started down the controlled street, pausing at the windows of the shops that didn't have heavy wooden shutters closing them for the night. The shuttered stores seemed mostly to be food shops; the wooden shelves extending beyond the shutters toward the street still held a few withered grapes and some cabbage leaves. Every time a car passed Allegra had to plunge with the few other night pedestrians into a deeply set doorway. When she decided she had had enough of dodging—walking downhill on the cobblestones was difficult enough without these mad leaps—she started back.

At the top of the hill, across the open space where the traffic light held back the cars, she saw a gateway in the high wall that had been on her left as she came up the other side of the hill she was climbing now. The gate made a dark frame for a lighted interior that, as she approached, became graveled ground. Its bridge led over a dry moat to an arched entrance between tremendously high towers topped with peaked slate hats—another fairy-tale setting. The old stone of the great walls looked yellow and warm under huge floodlights.

By contrast, the wall separating the towers from the street made shadows so deep they covered half the graveled space and so dense they seemed impenetrable.

A little shiver of fear shook Allegra. This was a fine spot after dark either for lovers or murderers. She hadn't gone fully inside the gate. Now she stepped back toward the lighted street. She would certainly keep Olive away from here at night—it was an ideal place for another one of her accidents.

The lighted walls and turrets beyond the gate were gorgeously theatrical, doubly gorgeous because you knew it wasn't painted scenery. However, Allegra was glad to leave the shadows behind her and return to the everyday street where everyday people walked. Though what was everyday about any street in Carcassonne? With all these stone buildings and walls, the cobblestones to walk or drive on, the tips of towers in sight beyond the houses, it was about the least everyday of any city she had ever been in. It was the people who were everyday and perhaps only the tourists. Wouldn't living in a place like this influence those who lived there? But how—make them more contemplative than other people, more aware of a sense of history and being part of it themselves, make them live in the past?

They weren't all living in the past, that was for sure. In the deep shade of a dark slit of side street she saw a pair of lovers, the man's arms wrapped about the woman, hers about the man. Allegra tripped on a cobblestone when she recognized the girl's dress.

It was Margot. And the man... they swayed just enough that Allegra could see the back of his head. The man was Henri.

Allegra moved on quickly, smiling. How lucky she hadn't fallen flat on her face. With the thud and clatter of a dropped handbag and probably a grunt even if she'd managed not to cry out, that oblivious couple in the side street could do no less than pick her up. How embarrassing to find that one of her own tour-mates had been gawking at you so hard she'd missed her footing.

She passed the next side street cautiously. Who, she asked herself, did she expect to find there? Brian? And with whom? Margot was otherwise occupied. She hoped it wouldn't be Cicely, but Elmer seemed the type who'd keep a tight rein on his young and beautiful wife. Surely it wouldn't be

Winifred or Jen.

The night's bag of surprises was not yet empty, however. Allegra passed the last side street before the hotel without recognizing or seeing any more lovers. But she hadn't been in her room more than an hour before she knew she still couldn't settle down to read. Perhaps thinking of Cicely made her think of postcards. She could buy them at the concierge's desk no matter how late it was. There was always a night man available. Once more she picked up her handbag and opened the door.

Directly across the hall another door closed. Brian still had his hand on the knob with his robed back toward the hall. But that wasn't Brian's room. Allegra drew back before he turned and brought her door almost to a close. She didn't want the latch to click and give him the feeling of being spied on. Now, whose room...?

Because the door wasn't quite shut, she heard another latch click, the definite closing of a door farther along the hall. Brian must have reached his room, and she couldn't go out for her postcards without causing embarrassment. If she still couldn't remember whose room was directly across the hall from hers, by the time she got back she'd look it up on her list. She was getting to be a nosy old woman, she told herself. What business was it of hers whose room Brian had been visiting in the middle of the night?

But he hadn't yet reached his room. As she stepped out, she saw him still walking down the hall, not walking as she had watched him walk before—striding along like a masculine man who had nothing to hide. Tonight, he looked sneaky, the only way she could regard that ultra-cautious progress as if he were doing his best not to be heard.

Allegra closed the door again. The postcards could wait; the list couldn't. Or at least she couldn't wait any longer to see it. Making out a room list was something she had heretofore regarded as a nuisance, a way for Olive to be able to lay her finger on any of her guests at any time. It had been one more chore for Allegra, but now it was about to pay dividends.

The list was on the writing table where she had made it out after the rooms were assigned this afternoon and left it for Olive.

Allegra picked it up and gave a little gasp.

"It can't be," she said aloud.

According to the list, the room across the hall was Winifred's.

She began to laugh, smothering the sound so she wouldn't wake Olive. Of all the tour group, Winifred seemed the least likely candidate for romance. It wasn't that she was ugly or had a bad figure, or even that she was six or eight years older than Brian. It was just that she seemed totally without sex appeal, even more than poor old messy Jen. But what did another woman know about sex appeal? Perhaps that starched efficiency of Winifred's was what Brian wanted. Come to think of it, she must be his type. He'd taken her out several times in Cincinnati, according to Olive.

Anyway, both of them could thank their lucky stars that Olive hadn't seen him coming out of Winifred's room tonight. That would have been more than enough to make Olive stage a new will-writing scene. Even the persuasive Brian wouldn't be able to talk his way out of a complication like this, his way or Winifred's either.

Chapter Eleven

Over their morning croissants, brioches, and coffee, Olive complimented Allegra on her industry of the night before.

"Such a large stack of cards," she said. "You must have been up half the night."

"I had trouble sleeping," Allegra said. "How's your ankle this morning?"

"Seems to be nearly all right," Olive said. "But don't spread the good news, since that's my excuse for staying those two extra days."

Why didn't Olive want anyone to know she was expecting a cable? They wouldn't know what was in it.

"Do you think you'll join today's sightseeing?" Allegra asked. "Driving over to the new town won't be strenuous, and you can do as much or as little walking around here in the old Cité as you like. Brian was going to take us in to the cathedral and the chateau, and then everyone was going to poke around the shops and little streets to suit themselves."

"That's fine for the rest of you," Olive said. "I think I'll stay here with my feet up. If I feel like exercise after everyone's gone, I'll take it then."

Olive did like her little secrets, such as concealing the improvement of her ankle. But maybe she was wise. If she stayed in her room, at least she wouldn't be involved in any more accidents. And it wasn't as if she really cared about seeing Carcassonne, or any other place. Allegra sometimes felt like Olive only traveled to Europe because it was the fashionable thing to do.

"Allegra," Olive said sharply, "isn't that someone at the door?"

It was only nine o'clock. One of the side delights of this trip was that, unless they had to leave early to reach a certain place at a certain time, no one felt rushed. They could enjoy leisurely breakfasts in bed as Allegra and Olive were doing now, or get up and go exploring on their own, but they never tried to get together until ten or later. Blast Brian, couldn't he have waited for his daily conference with Olive?

But it wasn't Brian at the door this time. It was one of the hotel maids, although not the glamorous, pert French-maid type of the American stage. This was a middle-aged woman with a good deal of facial hair and sharp black eyes set close together.

"Le concierge 'e say you 'ave *les habit*—'ow you say? Dress? To make clean," she said.

The two American women stared back blankly.

The French woman tried again.

"You fall, Madame. You get—" She made brushing motions with both hands against her uniform.

"Brian must have told the concierge you fell, and your suit needs cleaning," Allegra said. "If they can clean it here, we'd have plenty of time, with those two extra days."

"It needs a lot more than cleaning," Olive said. "Get me the suit I wore in Nîmes, will you, Allegra. The plaid one…"

Allegra took out the suit Olive had been wearing when she slid down the Colosseum steps. Woven in Scotland and tailored in America, it was a lovely soft wool with intermingled lines of red, yellow, green, and brown. One of the red lines of the jacket sleeve had been scraped completely out by the stone steps from the wrist almost to the elbow.

The French woman made a rapid tut-tutting noise and raised both hands heavenward.

"Maybe it could be rewoven while we're here," Allegra said. "The French are supposed to be very clever at that sort of thing. It's such an unusual plaid, and such lovely material. It might be worth a try."

"I don't think there's a prayer, Allegra, partly because it's such an unusual plaid," Olive countered. "And the damage is so extensive. I wouldn't want a botched job. I wonder—she looks about my size. If your French is equal to it, tell her she can have it."

"Madame gives *ceci a vous*," Allegra said, fumbling for words in two languages. "*Peut-etre vous* can mend it."

The chambermaid's black eyes brightened. She took the jacket and reached for the skirt.

"*Merci, Madame, merci*," she said.

"Wait," Olive said, holding up the skirt. "Maybe this will be all right to wear with blouses around the house."

Allegra felt more embarrassment than amusement. The chambermaid stood with one arm clutching the jacket, the other slowly coming back to her side. Her dark face looked darker, perhaps because her heavy black brows had drawn together.

"Oh, Olive, the skirt's bad too," Allegra said. "See, there on the side where it scraped along the steps. Stone doesn't do anything for wool."

Olive pursed her lips and looked more closely.

"I don't think you'd be happy wearing it," Allegra whispered softly. "It's not—perfect anymore."

Olive folded the skirt briskly.

"You're right, Allegra," she said. "I'd always remember what a beautiful suit it was once, and I'm afraid I'd think about that ghastly fall—headfirst down those stone steps."

Olive shivered and held out the skirt to the French woman.

This time no go-between was needed. The maid's hand went out as soon as Olive started to fold the skirt, and her heavy brows no longer met.

"*Merci, Madame*," she said again, and was in the hall before Madame could change her mind.

"My stockings were a total wreck, so I threw them in the wastebasket in Nîmes," Olive said. "I wonder if she could have mended them."

"I doubt if anyone could retrieve them," Allegra laughed, "but if it's possible I'm sure the people in Nîmes could do it as well as the people here. You want the first bath, Olive?"

By half past ten, Allegra found all the other members of the tour gathered in the long narrow hall near the outside door.

"How's Olive?"

"Where's Olive?"

"Is Olive's ankle worse?"

"She thought she'd take it easy for a while," Allegra told them. "But she'll join us for lunch."

Jen detached herself from the group. "I wonder if she'd like me to sit with her? I'll have plenty of time to see Carcassonne if we're going to be here a few days."

"I think she might take a nap," Allegra improvised quickly, although she told herself she was being silly. Jen, of all people, who had known Olive all her life. Why, Allegra and Olive could remember when Jen was born.

"Then I'd better not disturb her," Jen said. "I'll see the town now too. Where are we going first, Brian?"

They went into the cathedral across the square. Allegra might as well have stayed in the hotel for all the sightseeing she did that morning. She went with the others, knew when they were in the cathedral and when they were in the chateau, and when they were walking through the streets. At least she could tell the difference. But she didn't really see anything except the people she was with.

Both Winifred and Jen seemed to be jockeying for the place next to Brian, and they weren't satisfied with one on each side. Each wanted Brian's exclusive attention. And didn't Winifred have a slightly proprietary air? She would, naturally, after last night. But maybe she'd always had it and Allegra only noticed it because of last night. Whose door had closed, as Brian tiptoed down the hall?

The night before, Allegra had told herself she was getting to be a nosy old woman; not getting to be, she corrected herself, she'd arrived. At least earlier her nosiness had been directed toward protecting Olive. Then the thought of last night and its human implications gave way to the old worry about Olive and her will.

Presently Allegra realized that the group was breaking up.

"Okay, girls, descend on the shops," Brian said.

"Oh, look at that sexy enamel jewelry!" Cicely caught Margot's arm.

"Those square yellow earrings are terrific," Margot said. "Let's see how much they are."

The two girls went into the old stone shop. Elmer ducked his head at the low door and followed.

"There's some really good jewelry down toward the hotel," Winifred said. "Why bother with that costume stuff?"

As usual, Winifred's tone was annoyingly superior.

Henri's eyes were on the shop Margot had gone into while Jen's were on Brian. She had her hand on his arm before he could move away and began to say something she seemed earnest about. Intense as her voice seemed to be, it was low, and Allegra wasn't close enough to hear.

"Coming, Allegra?" Winifred asked, tapping her pink patent leather sandals on a cobblestone.

"Go ahead, Winifred, I may see you there," Allegra said. "I want to pick up some fruit while I'm here where the groceries are."

Jen and Brian had moved down a narrow side street. With no shops in that direction, Allegra could hardly follow. Anyway, what they were talking about was no business of hers, unless it had something to do with Olive and her will.

Standing in the middle of the street, looking in every direction, she could now see only strangers. Even Jen and Brian had disappeared. Henri was no longer watching the shop that sold the "sexy enamel jewelry." Did that mean that Margot had come out and they had gone someplace together? Were Cicely and Elmer still inside? Winifred had started toward the hotel; she said the shop with the good jewelry was in that direction. There were some shops down that way; Allegra had seen them in a bemused sort of way. But was Winifred there, or had she kept on going while Olive was alone in the hotel?

"Good Lord," Allegra said to herself, "she's Olive's first cousin."

But what difference did that make when it came to money? Distances were so short in this tiny walled city, any of her "nearest and dearest" might have beaten Allegra back to the hotel—with Olive there alone.

Once this thought occurred to her, none of them could have beaten Allegra to the hotel.

Chapter Twelve

When she got there, Olive was in the long hall downstairs, ready for lunch.

"There's a nice garden here on the other side of the building, with tables and chairs and umbrellas," Olive said. "It seems to be built right on top of the wall, and there's a view of—"

"My God, Olive, don't go out there!" Allegra cried. "One little push, and that would be the last of the so-called accidents."

"Let's not be unnecessarily dramatic, Allegra," Olive said. "After what's already happened, you can be sure I won't go near the edge when any of my guests are around."

Her guests were beginning to trickle back through the door from the square. Winifred first, then Jen without Brian.

"When I was in the garden this morning, they were all out," Olive said, her voice too low for even the advancing Winifred to hear.

"But they could have come back," Allegra said. She felt she was hissing, like the heavy in a melodrama.

Winifred looked pretty. She was wearing what Allegra thought of as her frivolous outfit—a pink drip-dry that matched her patent leather sandals. Her cheeks were pink, too, and she had that warm look again. Last night had done wonders for her. Funny, if she hadn't seen Brian coming out of Winifred's room, Allegra would have thought Winifred was too strait-laced for that sort of thing. Maybe it was the French influence. Anyway, she'd better not let Olive find out, or her name would be stricken from Olive's all-important will.

The Andersons and Margot were coming in now. Henri was wise to stay away from Margot while Olive was around.

"Did you find any jewelry you wanted, Winifred?" Allegra asked.

"There was a beautiful pink tourmaline pin I'd love to have, but the woman wanted too much for it," she said. "If I go back, in a few days I think I'll be able to talk her down. Don't you think that's the smart thing to do, Olive?"

As Olive agreed, Brian arrived, and they went in to lunch.

Discussing their projected visit to the new town across the river, Brian said, "Why don't you come with us this afternoon, Olive? You could stay in the car when the rest of us get out. Not that it's much to see compared with the Cité, but it's a pretty little town, and it'd be something for you to do."

"Thanks, Brian, but I think I'll stay put a while longer," Olive said. "I'll see you when you get back."

Allegra was the last one onto the bus. After her fright this morning, when they had all disappeared, she was going to make sure no one stayed behind.

They traveled back through the narrow street between the walls, the two near-squares, the narrow street of shops with tourists jammed into the doorways to let the bus pass, the incredible drawbridge, until they were out of the walls.

"Turn and look back when we get to the river," Brian told them. "There's an especially good view of the Cité from the bridge."

There was the dream city again—Carcassonne with its battlements and towers—but instead of seeing the beauty and romance of the ancient fortifications, all Allegra could see was how high the walls were. All she could think was that if someone were near the edge and someone else gave a push...

Presently they were driving through normally wide streets again, where there were more local people on the sidewalks than tourists.

Henri stopped the bus in the business district, and everyone got out.

"Why don't we all scatter?" Brian suggested. "If you're interested in shopping, you'll be a lot more independent alone than if we're one big happy family. Let's plan to meet at the bus in an hour."

Allegra stood on the sidewalk, watching the scatter process. Margot went off with Cicely, trailed by Elmer. They looked in windows as they walked slowly along the street, then all three turned in at one of the doorways. Brian went in the other direction, walking briskly as if he had an agenda. Jen and Winifred crossed the street with an air of not being together, an air that was verified on the other side by their prompt separation. Winifred went into a jewelry store directly across the street from the bus, while Jen walked slowly down the block and turned at the first intersection.

Allegra had decided to start out in the direction Brian had taken when a quick motion across the street caught her attention. She saw Winifred dart out of the shop she had gone into and beckon to a passing taxi.

What was she up to? Allegra heard the taxi driver's shrill voice, "La Cité? Oui, la Cité."

"My God—Olive—where can I find a taxi?" Allegra said.

"I will take you, Madame. Come," Henri said from behind her. Holding the coach door open, he reached for her arm.

It wasn't until she was in the bus, and they were turning around that Allegra realized what had happened. "Henri, you speak English!"

"A little, Madame," he said. His smile was completely charming. No wonder Margot was attracted.

"Does anyone else know you speak English?" Allegra asked.

"Mademoiselle Margot—" Henri began.

"Of course," Allegra said.

"And Brian," Henri said. He pronounced Brian with both syllables equally accented in the French way.

"Did you know Brian before this trip?" Allegra asked.

"Oui," Henri nodded. "One summer I drive French families in England for the tour bureau of Brian."

"When he was there two years ago?" Allegra said.

"Oui," Henri said again. "The summer we met Mademoiselle Wallace. And then we meet again—Brian and I—in Paris."

"This summer?"

"Oui, Madame."

"Why didn't you let us know you spoke English?"

"So little, Madame." Henri said. "Brian thought it would be better. More fun for you ladies."

Brian would, thought Allegra. Brian, the schemer. It would suit his plans very well. A regular spy system. Brian's pleasant smile, his mischievous wink, his brisk walk that barely missed being a swagger—was she being unfair? Was this more coincidence? Just because a man had the same sense of humor she had, didn't make him any less a con man and a schemer. There were too many coincidences connected with Brian, just as there were too many coincidences connected with Olive's accidents. Was Brian behind those too?

"*Regardez, Madame,*" Henri said. "The taxi of Mademoiselle Jenkins—it is ahead."

"Henri, you're wonderful," Allegra said.

She hoped this charming young man wasn't part of the scheming, but merely a tool in the scheme.

"It was kind of you to bring me right over," she added. "If I'd had to wait to find a taxi…"

"You feel you must hurry, Madame," Henri said. "I understand. Mademoiselle Margot, has tell me you worry about Madame Wallace."

"Well, yes," Allegra agreed. "Wouldn't you, after those two accidents?"

Henri nodded slowly.

"*Oui,*" he said. "They may have been accidents. They may not. Madame Wallace is fortunate that you are here, Madame. To have so good a friend…"

Allegra felt pleasantly warm. She didn't wonder Margot liked this young man.

"Do not be alarm, Madame," Henri said. "We arrive as soon as Mademoiselle Jenkins."

And they did, though it was nip and tuck at the drawbridge. Henri had to run the red light right on the rear bumper of the taxi. The car behind them honked angrily, but there was no official to stop them.

Allegra got out of the coach while Winifred was paying the taxi driver in front of their hotel.

She looked astonished upon seeing Allegra and Henri.

"Why did you come back?" Allegra asked at the same time Winifred asked,

"What's the matter? Why did the bus—"

They both stopped at the same time.

The second time Allegra started first.

"Why did you come back, Winifred?" she asked again.

"I saw the same pin I looked at this morning in a jewelry store across the street from where the bus parked," Winifred said. "It was three and a half dollars more than the one here, so I rushed right back to get this one before the woman sold it to someone else. If I'd only known the bus was coming it would have saved me taxi fare. You must have been right behind me. What did you and Henri come back for?"

"I developed a splitting headache, and since we weren't going to use the bus for an hour there was plenty of time for him to bring me home," Allegra said.

Either she wasn't as inventive as Winifred, or Winifred was telling the truth. But she'd stopped at the hotel, not the shop. She probably didn't know the name of the shop. And how could she tell someone in a language she didn't know to stop at a shop she didn't know the name of? The shop was only a block or two from the hotel anyway.

"Well, I mustn't stand here talking," Winifred said. "That pin might be sold right under my nose." She started back the way they had come.

The taxi had already gone. Henri, lifting his hand in a farewell gesture, turned the bus around and left too.

Feeling deflated and a little silly, Allegra went into the hotel.

Olive wasn't in their room. Already unstrung, Allegra was shaken. She dashed down to the desk.

"*Madame Wallace—?*"

The concierge pointed toward the terrace garden, the garden on top of the wall.

And there she was. She was standing on the drop-off side of the garden looking out over the rolling hills and vineyards and the new town across the river.

"Olive!" Allegra cried.

Olive gave a startled jump and moved back two or three steps before she turned around.

"Goodness, Allegra, you scared me!" she said. "I didn't know it was you, and then—"

"Then you remembered what I said about not going near the edge," Allegra said. "I could have been someone else—someone who wanted to cause another accident."

Olive walked over to a table near the wall of the hotel and sat down.

"Let's have a cup of tea," Olive said. "I think we both need it." She beckoned to a waiter hovering in one of the doorways.

"I thought you were going to stay in the new town most of the afternoon," she added. "Was it that uninteresting?"

"I've no idea," Allegra admitted. "I didn't even see it except driving through. We had barely gotten out of the bus when I saw Winifred flag a taxi to come back here, and I thought about you here alone and that high wall… and… and… I followed." She gestured toward the outside edge of the terrace where Olive had been standing.

Now, why didn't she tell Olive that Henri had offered to bring her home in the bus? That they'd talked—in English—all the way back? That Henri had known Brian when Olive "discovered" him in England two years ago? How well had they known each other then? Was it only happenstance that they met in Paris this summer?

If she told, Olive might be angry enough to fire Henri right on the spot. Allegra didn't think Olive would fire Brian for his part in the Henri-Brian link any more than she had discharged him for selling information about her will. Brian could do no wrong.

Henri could. If he were gone, they couldn't get a substitute before it was time to leave for Biarritz.

All those reservations… Allegra shuddered.

And Margot—the trip would be spoiled for her without Henri. One could hardly expect a substitute to assume all of Henri's privileges as well as his duties.

"What happened to Winifred?" Olive asked. "If she came back, I haven't seen her."

"She said she could save three dollars and a half on that pin she looked at yesterday," Allegra said. "I know Winifred's a bargain-hunter, but I didn't know she cared that much for jewelry."

"She certainly wears very little—just her mother's plain gold wedding band on her own right hand," Olive said. "And the cameo pin that belonged to some aunt."

"Maybe she's a secret jewelry lover," Allegra said. "Anyway, when I last saw her, she was going in the direction of the shop where she saw that pin this morning. It didn't occur to me that she could be coming back for any reason except to get at you while you were alone and unprotected. And I wish to God, Olive, that you'd stay away from this terrace!"

"Both of the 'accidents' happened when everyone was present," Olive reminded her.

"Of course, or they might not be regarded as accidents," Allegra said. "It spreads the responsibility around. But when they get down to serious business..."

"I really think we've been making mountains out of molehills," Olive said. "Civilized people don't do that sort of thing."

"No? Then why are you afraid to have a room by yourself—on this civilized tour?" Allegra asked.

Olive's funny little smile quirked her lips.

"I was trying to save money," she said.

"Like hell you were," Allegra said. "I could tell you were afraid when you told me that day after the accident in Avignon that I was the only one you could trust."

"I was nervous after landing in the river," Olive explained. "It was quite a shock, you know."

"And what about falling down the stairs in Nîmes?" Allegra said. "Will it take another 'accident' to make you decide someone's really out to get you?"

"But those accidents weren't fatal, Allegra," Olive insisted. "They just scared me."

"They could have been fatal, and you know it," Allegra said. "You can't swim. If Henri hadn't gone into the river after you—"

"Then someone else would have," Olive said.

"Maybe not in time," Allegra said. "Don't you see how a little difference—a difference in the time you were in the water at Avignon or a difference in how you landed on those steps in Nîmes—you could have broken your neck, you know, or cracked your skull on those stone steps—that difference could have literally been the difference between life and death for you?"

"Hm-m-m," Olive murmured.

Allegra rushed on, "And here—if you fell off that wall on the other side of this terrace—if you fell off any of these high walls of Carcassonne—that's the kind of accident that would be bound to be fatal. All it would take is one good push."

"Sh-h," Olive said. "Here's the waiter."

She took a sip of tea, made a face, and said, "The French are such wonderful cooks. Too bad they can't make good tea. I wonder what's keeping Winifred."

"She'd jolly well better show up with that pin," Allegra said grimly. "No matter what it costs her."

"If they find out how much she wants it, it'll cost her plenty," Olive said. "Here she is now."

Winifred was coming through the doorway from the hall.

"I told her I came back because I had a headache," Allegra said softly. "If she asks how it is, don't say 'What headache?'"

"The concierge said you gals were out here," Winifred said. "I wanted to show you the lovely pin I got for so much less than I'd have had to pay in the new town. It's eighteen carat gold and a real tourmaline. The pink ones like this are rather rare. Isn't it terrific with my pink outfit?"

Winifred really was pretty when she let go of that iron control. Standing with her chest outthrust to admire the pin, looking happy and relaxed, she wasn't the prototype of an old maid, any more. Was this all last night's doing? Now it wasn't hard to see how Brian could be interested.

Allegra smiled at her.

"Pretty sexy, as Cicely would say," she said.

Winifred flushed.

Perhaps that wasn't the most tactful word choice, in view of last night. And let's hope Olive never finds out, Allegra thought, in case they're planning a repeat. Her mind swung back to the click of a latch she had heard last night. There wouldn't necessarily have to be a repeat for Olive to find out.

But the next hotel room door she saw closed by someone who wasn't the tenant of the room was Brian's. And the person who closed it was Jen.

Chapter Thirteen

The tour of the new town was over, and everyone was back in the Cité. Cicely and Elmer were still out on the cobblestones. Margot and Henri were too. Allegra had seen both couples on her usual trip to the post office for Olive. The others, she supposed, were back at the hotel taking naps or washing clothes or writing postcards or one of the scores of things you did in a slack moment on tour. When Allegra saw them, Margot and Henri had been sitting on a bench in the shade holding hands. They weren't doing much talking. Why should they? Besides, if Henri wanted to preserve the French-only illusion, he'd have to be careful about who was around when he spoke and in what language. Maybe their feet were tired. Even the young get tired feet, and they wouldn't be able to sit down to rest in the hotel together—not Olive's chauffeur and her prospective heir.

Elmer looked as if his feet were tired too, but he kept plodding after Cicely or stood, shifting his weight, while his wife examined the trinkets in the shops. Poor Elmer... although he wasn't really "poor Elmer"; he was too crazy about his young and beautiful wife to be pitied. But he was middle-aged, and the heat and cobblestones were getting to him.

Allegra had returned and was on her way down the hall to her room when Brian's door opened and Jen came out. Allegra nearly bumped into her. She was wearing her glasses, but acted as if she didn't see Allegra at all. It wasn't the starry-eyed look Jen used to have after a tete-a-tete with Brian that blinded her this time. But it was certainly some emotion, some *strong* emotion.

Allegra said, "Hi," rather weakly, while Jen stood there batting her eyes.

Finally she shook her head, said, "Oh, hello," and walked on down the hall.

She looked, Allegra thought, excited, but there was something else, something like triumph in her expression. She even walked with a sort of swing, as if she'd won a battle; it was not the way Jen usually walked, scurrying along in a self-effacing sidle.

It was seven o'clock when Brian came in to see Olive. Margot and both the Andersons were with him.

"What's this, a delegation?" Olive asked.

"Exactly." Brian's attractive smile flashed.

"Jen and Winifred would have come too, but they're both in the middle of changing," Margot said.

"But they completely agree with us," Cicely said.

"About what?" Olive demanded.

Brian was the spokesman.

"About your holing up in your room," he said. "You need some exercise, and there's an excellent restaurant on the street coming up from the drawbridge that they say serves the best cassoulet in town."

"That's too far to walk," Olive objected.

"We wouldn't expect you to walk. Brian says—" Margot began.

Brian interrupted Margot.

"We'll drive to the place where the cars line up for the traffic light," he explained. "Henri'll park the bus in that square, and we'll walk to the restaurant from there. It's only a few doors down from the street, and you'll have three good right arms to choose from."

"Three?" Olive looked from Brian to Elmer.

"Henri," Brian said. "He's both strong and willing, as you should know."

"When he pulled you out of the river," Margot added. She was going to see that Henri got full credit.

"What's cassoulet?" was Olive's next question.

"Don't hedge, Olive," Brian said firmly. "Cassoulet is something worth trying. It's a wonderful regional dish made of beans and sausage and goose and lamb and what-have-you. Some places make it better than others, but they say Blanche de Castile is particularly good."

"It sounds so—hearty," Olive said distastefully.

"What's wrong with hearty food now and then?" Brian said. "You're trying to talk yourself out of going, Olive, and you know it. My dear—"

Brian's smile was particularly winning, with the slightest touch of tenderness, Allegra decided, no more than the right amount for a young man toward an older woman who was his employer.

"—we think we know what's best for you," he continued.

"Besides, Olive dear," Jen said from the doorway, "we want you to enjoy this beautiful trip too. You're giving us such a wonderful time, an opportunity some of us, anyway, would never have if it weren't for you."

Trust Jen to get in her sickening two-bits' worth, Allegra thought.

"I don't know about the rest of you," Margot said matter-of-factly, "but I'm dying to try that cassoulet. Brian's got me drooling."

"They say it's delicious," Cicely murmured.

"Why don't you all go and I'll eat here in the hotel?" Olive suggested.

"That's exactly what we don't want you to do, Olive," Brian protested. "Can't you see—?" His voice evaporated as she turned away.

"I haven't heard you say anything, Allegra," Olive said. "What do you think?"

Allegra shrugged. She was certainly getting more French by the minute.

"It's entirely up to you," she said. "I'd like to taste cassoulet before leaving Carcassonne, but we can probably get it at the hotel."

"Allegra!" Winifred was at the door now beside Jen. "That's no way to cast a deciding vote. I thought everything would be settled long ago and I was going to be late. What's keeping us?"

"Let's go!" Elmer said. "Take my arm, Olive."

They all streamed out of the hotel and into the coach. Olive limped noticeably and gave Allegra a moment's concern before she realized Olive was simply demonstrating her need to stay in the hotel.

The coach jiggled over the cobblestones to the small square where the traffic light stood. There they left the bus and began to walk. On the way down the narrow thoroughfare, it was possible to walk three abreast only in the middle of the street, and only during the few minutes' pause in the stream of traffic before it was reversed as the light changed. When cars passed, Olive's party had to press themselves into doorways with the other foot traffic. The apertures before the doors, precisely the width of the thick stone walls, were usually too narrow to hold all nine members of the tour. Once Allegra found herself in one doorway while Olive was in another. Feeling she couldn't allow this to happen again, the next time cars came by Allegra crowded into the doorway where Olive was, already filled with four or five members of their own group and three or four strangers. It was so jammed she had to exert real push-power to avoid the cars, and she was inordinately relieved to reach the restaurant at last.

The cassoulet proved to be as good as its reputation.

As they all leaned back in their chairs, sighing with repletion although dessert was yet to come, Brian's smile was as satisfied as if he had been the chef.

"Now wasn't that cassoulet worth the effort?" he asked.

Olive's smile was like that of an indulgent mother for a precocious child.

"It was very good," she admitted.

"You were right about it being hearty, Olive," Winifred said. "If I ate like this often, I'd be out like this." She puffed out her cheeks. She was wearing the tourmaline pin and looked pretty again.

Jen laughed. She too looked more attractive than usual. She'd taken care with her dressing; her clothes weren't thrown on anyhow tonight, and she still had that look of assurance.

"I've already gained," she said. "I haven't been near a scale, but my skirts are getting tight."

"Not getting fat and finding hotel reservations are the two main problems of the tourist," Elmer said, almost back to his usual form.

Imagining that one of these people could possibly be plotting to do away with Olive seemed absolute nonsense. Here they were, sitting around the table, relaxed, saying the kind of things tourists say. These were people Allegra knew, most of whom she liked.

But when they were ready to leave, Allegra found she was tense.

Cars were still streaming through the narrow street—chugging uphill, then another set whooshing down. As each car passed, pedestrians made the usual dives for doorways. European drivers always seemed to drive like that, thought Allegra, with no regard for pedestrians, even when there was plenty of room. A tour bus came along. She could hardly breathe in the crush as everyone in the doorway squeezed back...

"Stop pushing!" That was Olive's voice.

"Look out!" someone yelled.

Olive was out in front of all the others, almost touching the moving bus. She screamed. She was falling under...

Before she went all the way, someone jerked her back.

In her sag of relief, Allegra almost went into the street herself. By now the bus had passed, but small cars were still whipping by on the downhill run.

"Olive!" Allegra cried as soon as she could speak. "Are you alright?"

"Thanks to Elmer," she said. "He pulled me back. They kept shoving from behind."

Elmer smiled wanly.

"Jen, you were right in back of me," Olive continued, her voice getting shrill. "You pushed me!"

Jen looked more shaken than Olive.

"I couldn't help it," she said. "I kept shoving back but I was being pushed harder. My God, Olive, think if—"

She stopped.

The two or three strangers in the group began to leave. A fat man remarked with forced joviality, "All's well that ends well. Glad you're okay, ma'am," and hurried to catch up with his own group.

"Let's get started," Olive said grimly. "I want to get out of this death trap before I really get done in."

"Done in!" Cicely cried. "But that means—"

Olive stared back. "Did I say done in? I should have said all in. Because that's what I am right now, and I want to get back to the hotel. Ready, Elmer?"

"Come on, Cicely," Margot said, giving her arm a tug.

With one hand clutching Elmer's arm, Olive's other hand went out to Henri. Brian, who was stepping forward, looked startled.

"We'd better get going," Winifred said. She took Brian's arm frozen outthrust, and they all followed the two girls and Olive with her escorts up the cobbled hill.

When Olive was safely in her room and Allegra had closed the door, the two women exchanged a long look.

Olive spoke first.

"You win," she said. "Someone must be out to get me. Three accidents are too many. This was a mighty near thing."

Allegra shivered. She kept remembering Olive almost under the big bus.

"It's so hard to know," she said. "The way they all happened, they could all have been real accidents. Or they could all have been—"

"Attempts at murder," Olive said briefly. Suddenly her voice became an affected soprano. "Oh, Grandma, what does 'done in' mean? That stupid Cicely!"

Allegra managed a weak smile.

"I'm sure no one thinks Elmer married her for her brains," she said.

"Elmer saved me tonight," Olive said. "Even if he did knock me into the river, he saved me tonight."

"You said Jen pushed you, Olive," Allegra said. "You don't really think—"

"I don't suppose she did it on purpose," Olive said. "It's hard to believe that of Jen. But she was certainly right behind me, and she certainly pushed. She was probably getting it from behind, herself, like she said."

"I definitely felt pushing against me," Allegra said. "The bus was so big and the space we were in so narrow, with so many people there it really could have been an accident."

Olive gave a snort of rejection.

"Do you know who was behind Jen?" Allegra asked.

Olive shook her head.

"That's the big advantage of an accident arranged to take place in a crowd, even a small crowd," Allegra sighed. "With a number of people bunched together, no one knows exactly where anyone else is or exactly what they're doing. Tonight, for instance, no one would put out his hands and visibly shove you. They can exert body muscles to push, and even the person next to them can't tell they're pushing in a group as tightly packed as ours was tonight."

"Well, there's always my private revenge," Olive said, her teeth clamped together. "If we only had an idea of who it was, I'd cut him out of my will. I know Jen pushed me, but the thought of her doing it deliberately is so unlikely I wouldn't feel right about cutting her out. Then there's Brian…"

"He was there, of course." Allegra looked thoughtful. "Though I don't know where he was in relation to you. You said he and Elmer had both let go of you while you were standing there?"

"Yes, we couldn't stand arm in arm with so many people," Olive said. "And the crowd itself held me up. But that wasn't what I meant. Remember how insistent Brian was about my going to this restaurant? He wouldn't take no for an answer. We may not be able to say who did what in a crowd, but we know who kept trying to get me where I could be put in the right position for the accident to happen."

"But Brian wasn't the only one urging you to go," Allegra said. "They were all pretty vocal about it. Maybe Margot was a little more insistent than the rest. And it was Margot who persuaded us to go to Avignon, Margot and Cicely."

"Well, I'm sure it wasn't Cicely or Elmer who did the dirty work tonight," Olive said. "I cut Elmer out of my will after Avignon, and they knew it. They'd have nothing to gain."

"There's another possibility, Olive," Allegra said. "The Andersons might have planned it tonight to give Elmer a chance to rescue you. They might have thought you'd be grateful enough to put Elmer back in the will."

"And that's exactly what I'm going to do." Olive walked to the writing table, took her yellow tablet out of the drawer, and pulled up a chair. "The only thing I'm hesitating about is Brian. If I'm going to cut him out, I'll do it at the same time."

"That's something you have to decide for yourself, of course," Allegra said. "But the Anderson bit… what we were saying… if they staged it to get back into your good graces, then…"

"Then there'll be another try later after I've had time to write a new will," Olive said. "A try without any rescue."

"There's almost bound to be another try later if we're right about these accidents, since none of them—" Allegra stopped.

Olive finished the sentence grimly. "Since none of them succeeded."

"Of course, we may be wrong about the accidents being attempts at murder," Allegra said quickly. "They may all have been genuine accidents and we're just a couple of old gals with too much imagination."

"You don't think that any more than I do, Allegra, do you?" Olive asked.

"Well..."

"Of course, you don't," Olive said. "Why don't you take a chair over by the door and if anyone knocks, deal with them. If you have to ask me something, fine. Only don't let anyone in till I get my will finished. I don't want anyone looking over my shoulder."

Olive would have been working on her latest will at midnight if she hadn't given Allegra instructions, because every one of her guests came to the door to ask how she was doing. Allegra let no one in, but each had a look at Olive busily writing. Most of them remarked that at least she hadn't had to go to bed.

Winifred said, "You'd think she'd forget about letters for one night."

Margot added, "She's got plenty to put in her journal tonight. If I came to Europe as often as she does, I wouldn't keep a journal. They're a nuisance."

The other visitors made no audible assumption about what she was writing. They didn't need to. Allegra could all but read the avid speculation in their faces. "Am I still in it?" "Who's she cutting out now?"

At last Olive gave a loud sigh and laid down her pen. "There, that's done." She began to tear up the old will.

"You're not going to put those in the wastebasket, are you?" Allegra asked.

Olive looked up, surprised.

"Where else?" she said. "But maybe you have something there. What'll I do with the scraps? Keep them in my handbag? Send them to my lawyer with the new will?"

"That's not a bad idea," Allegra said. "I was thinking of burning them."

"In what?"

"An ashtray, and you can flush the ashes down the toilet," Allegra said.

Olive laughed.

"Sounds like a spy novel," she said. "I doubt if any of our friends have equipment with them for recovering words from ashes, whatever that's called."

Allegra got up for the ashtray and together they completed the destruction of the will scraps.

Afterward Olive went to bed and promptly fell asleep, but the day had brought so much excitement that Allegra knew she would be awake for hours. And this was certainly no night to take a sleeping pill. She wondered if she would dare to take one again for the rest of the trip.

She got out her tour journal, but multiple nights of insomnia had brought it so nearly up to date that she ran out of material by two o'clock.

Still not sleepy, she decided to write to Bob Jr., and found the letter paper in the writing table drawer. Perhaps a little exercise would help her sleep. She was still fully dressed; she'd go downstairs and get a new supply from the concierge.

Wondering whether she'd run into Brian coming out of Winifred's room, Allegra kept her eyes and ears alert. All was quiet on the way down. When she returned with a handful of paper and envelopes, if she'd been walking in the middle of the corridor and thinking busily as she usually was, and if the hotel hadn't been so deeply still, she probably wouldn't have heard the voices. But she *was* walking close to the wall, approaching her own door, key in hand.

The night quiet of the hotel was so intense, it was almost spooky. In the stillness, the sound muffled by the door she was passing, she heard a man's voice. Startled motionless, she heard words through the panels.

"If you think—" the man's voice said distinctly. He mumbled something more, then came out loud and clear, "—you're nuts!"

It was Brian's voice. And the room was Jen's.

Allegra didn't want to hear any more. She hadn't meant to hear that. Hurrying to the next door, she tried to fit her key in quietly. They must be standing near the door, or their voices wouldn't have carried through. In her effort to be quiet, she dropped all the envelopes. She'd look fine picking them up on her hands and knees at the next door. The turn of the latch sounded like a fire alarm, but she got inside with all the envelopes and paper without being seen.

What in the world was Brian up to? Was he romancing both Winifred and Jen? It had been stated flat out that you could always find romance in Europe, but there was no Latin lover involved in this threesome. Allegra found herself chuckling. None of them needed to have left Cincinnati. But perhaps it was travel that started these things. When you get away from your home community...

But here she was, jumping to conclusions again. Maybe these night visits meant something other than romance. Brian's clear "You're nuts!" hadn't sounded exactly romantic. But surely any ordinary business wouldn't have to be conducted in private in the middle of the night.

Allegra gave up and began to write her letter.

Chapter Fourteen

"Y ou're going to Andorra today, aren't you, Allegra?" Olive asked over their breakfast trays.

"I'm not planning to," Allegra said. "I wouldn't enjoy it, worrying about you all the time. Unless you want to go yourself. Then I will."

"No, I'm going to stay home and rest," Olive said. "Last night gave me such a scare it really wore me out. If any of the others elect to stay, I really would appreciate your being here. But if they all go, you might as well have the trip too."

Before they had finished breakfast, Cicely Anderson came in. It was obviously early in the morning for her, too. She was wearing a filmy, fluffy, very feminine negligee over a filmy, fluffy nightgown, and it was easy to tell from Olive's expression that she didn't think Cicely was sufficiently clothed to be walking through the public hall.

In her pale green foam of chiffon, Cicely looked prettier than ever; the word that came to mind was *ravishing*. She also looked embarrassed. She kept stretching out her smooth brown legs and drawing them under her chair again, pulling at the ruffled hemline of her negligee as if it might cover them.

She had no more small talk than a man, and this morning couldn't even talk about postcards. Finally, as she had done the day she told Allegra about Brian's racket, she burst out with what was on her mind.

"Elmer and I have been talking—" she began. "Last night in that door-way—he was right in front with you and too busy trying to pull you back to see who was there. But I was toward the back and could see everybody.

82

It's a good thing it was one of those shops with more than usual space in front because our whole group was in it, every one of them, and three or four strangers besides. Jen was right behind you, though I'd hesitate to say she pushed you on purpose, because we were all pushing and shoving like nobody's business to keep from being squashed. You know—Elmer and I both think all these accidents can't be—accidental, if you know what I mean."

"I know what you mean," Olive said grimly.

"Elmer's tried and tried to think who might have tripped him in Avignon... but he couldn't find anything he could have tripped over like a rock or stick or root or anything," Cicely continued. "Remember how he hunted while we were there? When he couldn't find anything, he figured it must have been a person's foot, though it seemed funny nobody said anything. But then he thought, since Olive fell in because of it and got all wet and she's our hostess, that whoever he'd fallen over was embarrassed to admit it. But there's a better reason than that for not admitting it—if someone stuck out a foot on purpose. He even tried to remember who was near him when he got up, but he said his face was in the dirt at first, and by the time he stood up and began to brush off, everyone was over on the bank watching Henri rescue you."

"You didn't see anyone stick out a foot, did you, Cicely?" Allegra asked.

"No, I was having fun dancing, like Margot says the old song goes," Cicely said. "I wasn't watching for anything to happen. That was the first accident, you know, and I didn't know then there was anything to watch for. Now in Nîmes—"

Allegra leaned forward intently.

"In Nîmes?" Olive prompted.

"Well, you remember I was making a fool of myself with my umbrella. Winifred made me so mad..." Cicely paused again. "Well, it wasn't all my own doing. I made that first lunge, all right, but after that someone kept bumping into me and jogging my arm. We were all jumping around, and every time I turned to look there were three or four people behind me. I've been trying to remember who, but all I'm sure of is that they weren't always the same people. I remember seeing Winifred and Jen and once I saw you, Allegra, and Margot and Henri. Everyone was jumping around so much I don't think anyone was in the same place twice."

"But Margot and Henri didn't come up with us," Allegra said. "I clearly remember seeing them walk down that dim corridor under the arena before the rest of us went up the stairs."

"Then they must have come up when we were doing the gladiator act," Cicely said. "We'd have been too busy keeping out of the way of the umbrellas to notice. Because they were certainly there when you fell down the stairs. I nearly fell over Margot myself trying to get down to where you were, and I distinctly remember both of them behind me when my arm was jogged—one of the times it was jogged."

All three were still for a moment. Then Allegra said, "That accounts for nearly everybody."

"Everybody except Brian and Elmer," Olive said.

"Brian was always in front of me, of course, because we were dueling, or pretending to," Cicely said. "Our faces were always toward each other, but one minute our backs would be in one direction and one minute in another. He couldn't have jogged my arm. And I can't remember seeing Elmer at all."

Cicely lifted her round chin defiantly.

"Besides, he wouldn't have jogged my arm," she added. "He'd have been more apt to grab it to stop the silly nonsense."

Allegra looked at Olive.

"Did anyone jog your arm?" she asked. "Did you feel anyone bump you at all?"

Cicely's wide blue eyes, narrowed now, were as intent as Allegra's, both pairs fixed on Olive.

"I—can't—remember," Olive said slowly. "I guess it's something I've tried to forget."

"It might pay you to remember," Cicely said. This practical streak in Cicely never failed to surprise Allegra. With a thrust of smooth brown legs and a swirl of pale green, the glamorous blonde stood up. "Elmer and I wanted you to know what we thought about all these so-called accidents. If we're going to Andorra today, I'd better get dressed."

"Me too," Allegra said as she sprang out of bed. "Do you mind if I take the first bath today, Olive?"

She was putting on her stockings when the next visitor came—Winifred. Her face and hair looked freshly starched and ironed. She was neatly and what Allegra's mother would have called sensibly dressed in a navy drip-dry, completely without glamour.

Involuntarily Allegra exclaimed, "Where's your pretty pink outfit and the new pink pin? It's such a lovely sunny day for colors."

"They tell me Andorra's a shopper's paradise, like Hong Kong, with everything cheaper than where it was made," Winifred said. "Sometimes they up their prices if you look well dressed."

"That's using your head," Olive approved.

But Olive didn't know what Allegra knew. It wasn't bargains she was thinking of; it was Brian.

"Trying to look poor won't do you any good, Winifred," Allegra said. "As soon as you open your mouth, you're a rich American."

Winifred gave Allegra a don't-be-silly look and turned pointedly to Olive. "You're not going to Andorra, are you?"

"No, I'm—"

"I didn't think you would, so I wanted to run in before we left," Winifred said. "I've been worrying about what happened last night, and it made me think about what happened in Avignon and Nîmes."

"Yes?" Olive said encouragingly.

"Have you ever thought that—" Winifred stopped, then took the plunge— "that someone might be trying to kill you?"

Trust Winifred to call a spade a spade.

"What makes you think so?" Olive asked.

"Because any of those accidents could have killed you," Winifred said. "I guess you're just lucky, Olive."

A three-way silence fell, as it had when Cicely was there.

Allegra spoke first. She made her eyes as wide as Cicely's.

"But why would anyone want to kill Olive?" she asked.

Winifred gave her another of those don't-be-silly looks—this one more intense—and didn't answer.

"Why would you think that Winifred?" Allegra persisted.

At last Winifred said shortly, "Ask Olive." She was no longer calling a spade a spade.

Instead of asking Olive, Allegra continued to look at Winifred.

"But the only people who've been in on all the accidents are Olive's friends and relatives, our own little group," Allegra said. "She may have enemies, I wouldn't know, but surely not in this group."

Olive came to Winifred's rescue.

"I think I know what Winifred means," she said dryly. "Did you have anyone special in mind, Winifred?"

"Anyone special?" Winifred was thrown so much off balance by the question that for a moment she seemed as disorganized as Jen.

"The most likely candidate for who's out to get me," Olive prompted.

It was funny. Olive avoided using the word *kill*. Allegra avoided it. Even Cicely did. But Winifred didn't balk at saying *kill*.

"Didn't it strike you as odd—maybe significant would be a better word—that at Avignon you fell in the river because of something Elmer did, and at Nîmes you fell down the stone steps because of something Cicely did?" Winifred said.

"You're implying that the Andersons are responsible for these—accidents?" Olive asked.

"I certainly wouldn't point a finger at anyone," Winifred said virtuously, "if it weren't so obvious."

"Perhaps a little too obvious," Allegra objected.

"But what about last night?" Olive said. "It was Elmer who kept that from being an accident. It was Elmer who saved me."

"Cicely was behind you in the crowd in the doorway," Winifred said. "I know it was Jen directly behind you. But Cicely was behind her. I noticed because I was standing next to her. You said Jen pushed you. Well, Cicely was pushing her."

"How do you know?" Olive demanded.

"Jen said so," Winifred said. "I don't mean later, when everyone was trying to clear himself. I mean at the time. I saw Jen turn around and say, 'Don't push so hard! You're making me push Olive!'"

Again, the three-way silence fell.

Winifred broke it.

"You see what I mean, don't you, Olive?" she said. "The Andersons realized it looked bad to have them responsible for the first two accidents, so they got together on this one—Cicely fixed it so Elmer could save you."

"I was there too, Winifred," Allegra reminded her. "I know what a tight squeeze it was in that doorway. Everyone was pushing."

"Don't let Cicely do what the kids used to call a 'snow job' on you," Winifred said. "She can be a convincing talker, especially looking like she does."

Had Winifred seen how Cicely looked this morning in that pale green negligee? Had Winifred seen her come in and guessed what she came for? Winifred's room was right across the hall—as Allegra remembered well—and she didn't seem like the type to miss much.

Winifred stood up. "Well, I'd better get going."

"So had I," Allegra exclaimed, "or the bus will leave without me."

"I'll make sure Brian waits for you," Winifred said, with firmly imposed generosity. "Don't let anything I said upset you, Olive."

Allegra dropped her compact. Would being told that someone was trying to kill you be upsetting?

"I wanted you to be on the lookout," Winifred added as she closed the door.

"Well, what do you make of all that?" Olive asked.

"Trying to counteract whatever Cicely said," Allegra said, reaching for her handbag. Was it really all right to leave Olive? By herself, yes. But if anyone did what Winifred did yesterday... "Take care, Olive. If I see anyone sneaking back, I'll sneak back right along with them."

If anyone did leave the coach, thought Allegra as she climbed aboard, it would probably be before they got out of Carcassonne. Transportation back would be complicated once they were on the road. Complicated, but not impossible. There must be a public bus of some sort to bring the local people to Carcassonne, and once at Andorra, full of tourists, there might be any number of thumb-your-way rides to be hitched. She shouldn't have come. She couldn't watch everyone after they'd scattered for shopping.

The problem was solved when they stopped at the traffic light. Jen stood up.

"I've got to go back," she said. "Let me out, will you, Brian? I left my passport and I—I don't feel up to going to Andorra today. Or anyplace else. I feel terrible."

"You're not going to drop her here, are you, Brian?" Margot said, "Can't we turn around and drive her back? If she's sick..."

"Yours to command, my dear," Brian said. "It'll only take a few minutes. Henri—"

He chattered in French much longer, Allegra felt sure, than it would take to ask someone to turn around and go back to the hotel. He and Henri were keeping up the fiction, of course. She wondered if Brian knew it was no longer necessary as far as she was concerned. If she and Margot knew, maybe others too had found out.

When Henri stopped at the hotel, Allegra was right behind Jen.

"I've been having second thoughts myself," she said. "I don't feel so hot either."

"What is this—an epidemic?" Brian demanded.

"The Black Death strikes again," Elmer said cheerfully. "You feeling all right Cicely?"

As they stood at the hotel door watching the bus drive away, Allegra turned to Jen.

"Can I do anything for you?" She thought Jen looked as normal as she did, but this was another fiction to be kept up.

"Oh, there's nothing the matter with me," Jen said candidly. "I just thought this would be a good chance to talk to Olive alone."

"I hope I won't cramp your style," Allegra said. "I'm afraid I'm going to have to lie down." This was no time for Allegra to be candid, to let Jen know she wasn't trusted.

"I don't mind you, Allegra," Jen said. "In fact, it might be a good idea for you to hear. Anyway, I shouldn't be spending any more money, and I understand that's the main point in going to Andorra."

"Shoppers' paradise, the bargain basement of Europe," Allegra murmured.

"Exactly," Jen said. "Why put temptation in my way? I spent way over my Customs allowance in Nice as it is. And it isn't being duty-free that counts, it's the money itself. I simply can't afford it."

When Jen was being completely natural as she was now—not twittering with nervous gestures or buttering up Olive, or—heaven help her—being coy, she wasn't unattractive. If only someone had the nerve to tell her how to dress, or at least how not to dress and how not to act. But how could a grown woman tell another grown woman things like that?

When they reached the door to Allegra and Olive's room, Allegra knocked and called, "Olive."

When Olive came to the door, it was evident that she had just gotten out of the tub.

"What in the world?" she said. "Did Brian decide not to go to Andorra today?"

While Jen was explaining, Allegra remembered to walk over to her bed but forgot to lie down when she heard Jen say, "What I wanted to talk about was last night and the Nîmes accident and the Avignon accident. I don't think they were accidents. I think they were done on purpose—arranged—and they all fit together."

Olive pulled her robe more snugly about her and sat down in the guest chair. "What do you mean, Jen?"

"Last night—I know you felt me pushing but I couldn't help it; I was being pushed too hard myself," Jen explained. "And do you know who was pushing me? Cicely Anderson!"

Talk about gleaming eyes, Allegra thought. Gleaming glasses could be equally as alarming.

"I know it was Cicely," Jen went on, "because I turned around to tell her to stop and saw her. She had both hands against my back and was really shoving."

"You had to push, Jen, or be squashed in that crush." Allegra felt as if she had been through this a hundred times. But it really wasn't fair to accuse any one person of pushing when everyone had been pushing. Though it was entirely possible, all too possible, that one person had been pushing in a definite direction with a definite goal in mind...

"I'm telling you what I know," Jen said huffily, settling her glasses. "If you don't want to hear it..."

"Go on, Jen." Olive said impatiently. "Allegra's pointing out the other side of the coin. She's the lady with the blindfold holding the scales of justice. Did you see anything else?"

"I can't think of anything special last night," Jen said. "If anything should come to me later, I'll tell you. But have you thought about the way all these accidents fit together?"

"Fit together?" echoed Olive. "What do you mean?"

"Elmer caused your first accident and Cicely the second with that silly umbrella," Jen explained. "Now here it's Cicely again—"

"Don't forget it was Elmer who saved Olive last night," Allegra countered. "So that blows your Anderson theory sky high."

"No, it doesn't," Jen insisted. "What it means is there'll probably be another attempt—after Elmer's been put back in Olive's will."

Jen, too, could call a spade a spade. Though, interestingly enough, she and Winifred had been talking about different spades. Winifred hesitated at admitting it was a bequest Olive's guests were after, Jen at using the word *kill*.

Maybe Jen would know...

"When they came to our room yesterday to try to get Olive to go out for dinner, I gathered from the way Brian spoke that they all talked it over beforehand. Were you in on that conference?" Allegra asked.

Jen nodded.

"Do you know who suggested taking Olive?" Allegra said.

"Why, I think—" Jen began twisting her hair. "—I think it was Elmer. Now don't say—"

"This isn't speculation, Jen. I'm just trying to get at facts," Allegra said, looking at her sternly. "Are you sure it was Elmer?"

"Pretty sure. I think— no, maybe it was Margot." Jen was in her usual dither. Come to think of it, she hadn't dithered since yesterday when Allegra had met her coming out of Brian's room with that excited, triumphant look replacing her ordinarily vague expression.

"Or was it Cicely?" Jen was Jen again.

It was probably useless to ask, thought Allegra, but...

"Do you have any idea who suggested going to Blanche de Castile's in the first place?" she asked.

"I thought it was Brian," Jen said. "But maybe I jumped to that conclusion because he's always the one who finds out about interesting places and things to do. After all, he's the director."

Allegra laughed. "Yes, he is. He also speaks French."

"And he's been here before," Olive added.

"I'm sorry, Allegra, I don't know where the original idea came from," Jen said. "Brian brought it up when we were all down on the terrace having—"

Jen stopped. She looked from Allegra to Olive.

"—refreshments about six o'clock," she continued quickly. "But that doesn't necessarily mean it was his idea. It would be natural for him to propose it; as I said, he's the director."

"Yes, it would," Allegra agreed. "That's the trouble; everything's so natural it's hard to make yourself think these accidents can be anything but accidents."

"I know what you mean," Jen burst out. "That's what I thought too, at first, but after last night... I don't trust that Cicely. I don't think Elmer would have done it by himself. She put him up to it."

Having shot her bolt, Jen left.

"She and Winifred really have their hooks into Cicely, don't they?" Allegra remarked.

"Do you trust her?" Olive asked. "I don't."

"Trust her? N-no," Allegra said. "And yet—while I don't quite trust her, I find myself liking her. Sort of the way I feel about Brian. By the way, where was Brian in last night's melee? Elmer was on one side of you, but Brian wasn't on the other."

"No. I told you they had to let go of me in the crowd," Olive said.

"I don't think any of the girls mentioned him," Allegra said.

"They all said everyone was there," Olive said.

"But no one said where Brian was," Allegra said. "I'd like to know where he was in relation to where you were."

That ended the conversation. It was clear that Olive didn't want to talk about Brian. Did that mean she had cut him out of her will—or left him in? Well, it was certainly none of Allegra's business, and she wasn't about to ask.

The day passed quietly for the three members of the Wallace tour left in the walled city, though the tempo picked up at lunch. Olive insisted on being served on the terrace, not at a table against the inside wall this time, but right out in the middle. Allegra's story about feeling sick began to come true. Jen kept getting up and going over to the drop-off side, then calling to "dear Olive" to come to see something that couldn't be seen from the table. Though Olive kept responding to the clutch of Allegra's hand on her arm rather than to Jen's voice, what about the next time? Then Olive made Allegra feel like a dirty dog by smiling affectionately at both of them and saying, "It's good to be with old friends."

Every time Allegra leaned the conversation toward the events of the night before and Brian's position in the doorway, Olive said either, "We've already threshed that out," or, finally, "I don't want to talk about it anymore."

At last, the interminable lunch hour came to an end and the three women got safely back to their rooms.

The tempo picked up again when the others returned—hot, dusty, and loaded with packages. It began right before dinner with the arrival of Margot and Henri at Olive's door. Her eyebrows shot up disapprovingly when Allegra opened it. As a driver and as the possessor of a good right arm Henri was fine, as an escort for Margot he was not.

"Look, Olive," Margot began. Then she glanced down the hall. "May we come in?"

Margot and Allegra sat on the beds to leave a chair for Henri, but he remained standing.

The skirmishing over, Margot shook back her hair and began again.

"Winifred said she came in to see you this morning and, with Jen here all day—" Margot began. "They're both so prejudiced against Cicely I was afraid they might have told you all kinds of things about last night to influence you against her. It was Jen who was behind you, Olive, directly behind you. If you felt pushing, she's the one who did it."

"She and everyone else in the doorway," Allegra murmured.

"I was told that Cicely was the next one behind Jen," Olive said, her eyes narrowing. "Do you know anything to the contrary?"

"Well—" Margot turned to Henri. Brown eyes met brown eyes warmly, and a jumble of French and English passed between the two young people. "I'm not dead sure, because we were all so squashed in, but Henri says she was."

"So—"Olive began.

"So, she could have pushed Jen, right?" Margot looked distressed. "Crushed back the way we were and with everyone pushing to get room to breathe, it would be hard to say whether one person was pushing any harder than another."

"Can you remember who was behind Cicely?" Olive asked.

Margot shook her head and turned to Henri, who shrugged, palms turning out as his shoulders lifted.

"Or who was behind the person behind Cicely?" Allegra persisted.

Again, the mixed-language discussion, this one longer, with more gestures.

"If I understand Henri correctly," Margot told them, "he doesn't know whether there was anyone behind Cicely or not, but he says plenty of pressure could be exerted at an angle. Whoever pushed Olive wouldn't necessarily have had to be directly behind her."

"That leaves almost everyone on the hook," Allegra said, "as usual."

"Except Elmer," Margot said. "And speaking of Elmer—don't let Jen and Winifred talk you into believing that he deliberately stumbled to knock you into the river at Avignon or that Cicely deliberately made you fall downstairs with her umbrella-waving at Nîmes. Anyone could have taken advantage of the milling around and general confusion to make what happened happen and one of those so-called accidents might actually have killed you if Henri hadn't been right on the ball in Avignon, and Brian in Nîmes, and Elmer here."

She jumped up and headed for the door, talking over her shoulder and around Henri as she moved.

"I must show you the groovy watch I got in Andorra, cheaper than it would have been in Switzerland," Margot said. At the door she turned back briefly. "Please watch out, Olive! These don't look like accidents to me anymore, or to Henri either."

As the door closed behind them Allegra said, "Last night really shook everybody. I think I'll take a pill tonight and have a good sleep for a change."

"It shook me a little too," Olive said.

"It's interesting to see who's accusing who of what now that they're admitting those accidents weren't accidents," Allegra said.

"Everyone but Brian has had something to say." Olive paused. "He's coming up later; he told me he had some checking he wanted to do and asked me to wait up for him."

"It is funny," Allegra said, "with all the speculation and finger-pointing today, no one has put any blame on Brian."

Olive stiffened.

"Why should they?" she said. "I know we talked about his being too eager to get me to that restaurant, but we should have given him credit for thoughtfulness and interest in my welfare. He wanted to keep my ankle from stiffening and give me a change of scene. He's really a dear boy, Allegra."

"Ha!" Allegra said inelegantly. "Don't forget he started that umbrella business in Nîmes and no one's even mentioned it. He must have them all as mesmerized as he does you."

"Allegra! I take exception to that statement," Olive said. "If you can't recognize a person's worth without knowing all about his life and ancestry..."

"I'll be interested in seeing who he points his finger at," Allegra said. "That must be the dear boy knocking now." She rose to open the door.

When Brian came in, though he smiled at her as well as at Olive, and as warmly as usual, he went through the old routine—looking from Olive to Allegra and back to Olive again until Olive rose to the occasion and asked Allegra to take her book downstairs.

Her book was still in her hand. Stifling an impulse to throw it at him, Allegra stalked out. She'd be damned if she was going to sit down meekly and read while Brian was filling Olive up with God knew what lies. Lies or facts, they were something Allegra wanted to hear, and as Olive's protector she felt she needed to hear them.

Come to think of it—she stood in the corridor thinking of it—when she and Olive were talking about the various versions they had had of the "accidents," Allegra had wanted to know where Brian stood, literally where he stood, last night and in the Avignon accident. In Nîmes he had been one of the star performers, and Cicely had insisted he couldn't have jogged her arm. But that didn't mean he couldn't have maneuvered the direction of the duel in such a way as to bring Olive to the stairs and, with another lunge in that direction, down them. None of the others had even brought up his name when they were making accusations. Was that because he was in the clear, or were they protecting him? Jen and Winifred might, Henri and Margot might, Elmer almost certainly wouldn't.

Allegra squared her shoulders and decided she'd ask. She would ask them all. And now was a good time. It might be a little late, but Olive was the only early-to-bed one on the tour, and right now Olive was otherwise occupied. So now, as well as being nosy, Allegra was being spiteful. Brian had shut her out of her own room and away from the information he was supposedly giving Olive. But it really wasn't a matter of idle curiosity, she reminded herself.

She knocked on the Anderson's door. No response. She knocked on Henri's. No response there either. Margot's next. Still no response. They might have all gone out together. Though Carcassonne was hardly Marseilles, could there still be some nightlife here?

There were still Jen and Winifred, who were likely to be in.

Allegra knocked on Jen's door first.

A fluttery voice called, "Just a minute."

She shouldn't raise Jen's expectations.

"It's Allegra," she said. "It doesn't matter what you have on."

Jen opened the door about six inches, wearing the utilitarian robe she had bought for this trip in a dull color guaranteed not to show soil—or the woman in it. "Yes?" she asked uncordially.

"May I come in?" Allegra asked. "I want to ask you something."

"Well, I—" Jen hesitated.

"It'll probably require a long, complicated answer, Jen," Allegra said. "I don't think it's something we should discuss in the hall."

With obvious reluctance, Jen pushed the door wider open and let Allegra inside.

What was bothering her? Then Allegra remembered the man's voice last night. Maybe Jen was expecting Brian. On the bed lay the answer—a pale blue froth of nightgown and negligee as filmy and feminine as the pale green Cicely had worn this morning.

Like a mother grouse with the broken-wing technique, Jen kept trying to distract Allegra's attention from the bed. She seated her guest at the writing table with her back toward the bed and placed a chair for herself at the side of the table.

"What's the matter, Allegra?" She was twisting her hair again. "Has anything happened to Olive?"

"No, she's all right," Allegra said. "Brian's in there talking and they threw me out. There was something I forgot to ask you—"

"Why are they so private?" Jen interrupted. "Can't they talk with you there?"

"Maybe it's something about business," Allegra said. "They always throw me out when they have a business conference; after all, Olive's business is none of mine. I assumed Brian had something to say about last night since all the rest of you came in today to talk about it."

Jen looked distressed.

"I do hope no one... I tried to push her out into the street," she said. "I was being pushed so hard myself that I was being shoved right into her. But it wasn't my fault. That Cicely—"

"I don't think anyone would believe you did it on purpose, Jen," Allegra said. "What I wanted to know—I have a pretty good idea of where everyone was standing in that doorway except Brian. Nobody mentioned him at all. Do you have any idea where he was in relation to Olive?"

"Surely you don't think—" Jen said.

"I don't think anything specific," Allegra said. "But we need to know where everyone stood. It would help Olive to be on her guard if we had some idea of who she should look out for."

"Well, I don't think it's Brian," Jen said. "It'd be much more likely to be one of the people Olive's leaving lots of money to, like one of the relatives."

"You're thinking of Elmer, I suppose," Allegra said.

"Because of Cicely!" Jen said. "Otherwise, I'd never think anything like that of Elmer."

"Winifred and Margot are relatives too," Allegra pointed out.

"Y-y-yes," Jen agreed slowly. "But a woman—somehow they don't seem the type."

"Cicely's a woman and you think the worst of her," Allegra said. "Besides, the books say there is no type, and certainly there's no one on this trip I'd think of as a murderer type... except possibly Brian."

"Allegra! Brian's no murderer," Jen insisted. "And he wasn't anywhere near Olive last night."

"I thought you couldn't remember where he was," Allegra said.

"Well, I can't remember exactly," Jen said. "But I do know he wasn't near Olive. Why, you were nearer than he was."

Obviously, she was going to get nowhere on the Brian question. Allegra stood up and had one more look at the filmy things on the bed, which were no more like the cotton pajamas and heavy robe Jen usually wore than the robe she had on now was like Cicely's negligee. Allegra tactfully said nothing, and soon found herself standing in the hall again.

Jen's room, next to her own, gave her almost as clear a view of Winifred's door as she had had the night she saw Brian closing it. Even so, if she had not been looking at the door, for she was going to see Winifred next, she might not have seen it move. It had evidently been slightly ajar, and the faint click of the latch confirmed her feeling of motion.

Did that mean Winifred had come in? But where would she have been at this time of night? Or was she simply keeping an eye on anything that might be going on in the hall?

Allegra knocked softly.

"Who is it?" Winifred called. Another fiction to be sustained. As if she didn't know it was Allegra and where she had come from.

Allegra identified herself and the door opened.

She almost gasped. Winifred was wearing a negligee and nightgown set like the one on Jen's bed, only Winifred's was pink, and she looked pretty in it even though her cheeks were not pink tonight and her hair was as rigidly in place as it had been when she left for Andorra this morning. Were Jen and Winifred both expecting a visitor tonight? The same visitor? On the other hand, Allegra reminded herself, she didn't know Winifred's habits as she did Jen's. Maybe Winifred wore that alluring outfit every night.

"Forgive my knocking so late," Allegra said. "Brian's talking to Olive in our room, and I got thrown out, so I thought this was a good time to check on something about last night I'm not clear on."

"What something?" Winifred asked.

"Do you mind if I come in?" Allegra said. "I'd rather not be overheard."

Winifred seemed to be as reluctant a hostess as Jen, but not for the same reason. Whatever Winifred was concentrating on was outside her room; she left the door open, so Allegra's visit wouldn't make her miss it.

"What's your problem?" she asked, her eyes on the half-open door.

"I'm confused about where Brian was last night when the bus passed and we were all squeezed into that doorway," Allegra said.

"He was there with the rest of us," Winifred said.

"Yes, but where did he stand in relation to the rest of us?" Allegra asked. "I was in the front row and didn't see where anybody was except Olive and Elmer."

"I don't remember," Winifred said. "Seems to me he was somewhere behind you, but I didn't notice."

"I don't suppose you noticed where he was in Avignon either, when we were all dancing there under the bridge?" Allegra asked.

"I haven't any idea where anybody was that time," Winifred said. "No one even thought of an accident then, let alone something worse than an accident."

No one except one person, Allegra thought, the one trying to pull it off. The word *if* no longer entered into her speculations.

"I don't suppose you have any idea whether Brian was planning that umbrella duel in Nîmes, do you?" Allegra asked.

"Of course I don't," Winifred said stiffly. "How on earth would I know? Besides, how would he know Cicely was going to bring that silly long-handled umbrella? Or Jen her short one, for that matter?"

"It was threatening rain that morning, but no one else brought an umbrella..." Allegra mused aloud. "He could have asked Jen and Cicely to bring theirs."

"Oh, for God's sake, Allegra, why would he do that?" Winifred said. "What is this anyway—an unofficial investigation of Brian Gifford?"

So Winifred was through answering questions now too. Well, at least they had made her take her eyes off the door.

As Allegra left, her own door opened, and Brian came out. He looked surprised to see her with Winifred.

"Hi, gals," he said curtly, and walked down the hall toward his room.

Allegra hurried across the hall. "Who did Brian point the finger at, Olive?"

"The Andersons. Who else?" Olive said. "The only ones who haven't practically accused them are, of course, the Andersons themselves and Margot."

"And Henri," Allegra said.

"I'm sure I don't know what he thinks any more than I know what he says," Olive said, a look of annoyance on her face. "I have to rely on Margot's interpretation."

"You said Brian told you at dinner he had some checking he wanted to do before he talked to you tonight," Allegra said. "Did he tell you what he was trying to find out?"

"He wanted to ask Cicely and Jen whether anyone had suggested that they carry their umbrellas that day we went sightseeing at Nîmes, and if so, who," Olive said.

"What did they say?" Allegra asked.

"Cicely said she and Elmer and Jen, and Winifred were trying to decide whether it was going to rain while they were waiting for the rest of us in the coach—remember we had to shift our bags from those three or four different hotels to the Imperator before we went sightseeing?" Olive said. "Well, Brian and Henri were rounding up the separate porters and bags before they came to the hotel where you and I and Margot were staying, and it was then the vote was taken for or against umbrellas. Winifred was against. She insisted the weather was clearing. Jen was for and produced her folding umbrella from the outside pocket of her handbag. She said she'd had her hair done in Marseilles and was taking no chances. Cicely wavered but Elmer told her to take it because she might not find a hairdresser to suit her, till we got to Biarritz."

Allegra sighed. "So, we're really no further ahead than ever."

Chapter Fifteen

Olive was already out of bed and dressed when Allegra woke the next morning.

"What time is it?" Allegra asked sleepily. "I must have overslept."

"It's only eight o'clock," Olive said. "I woke up early and decided to write Foster McKane. Would it be awfully inconvenient for you to have your bath and breakfast later and take this to the post office? It's instructions he should have right away."

For Olive, this was almost saying *please*. And she almost gave an explanation, too. In any event, and even if it hadn't been a letter to her lawyer, Allegra couldn't say no.

She got up and dressed, feeling she was stumbling around with her eyes shut. These leisurely breakfasts in bed had spoiled her.

On her way through the narrow streets to the post office, Allegra pressed both shoulders against the wall to get out of the way of a police car tearing in the direction she had come from, its siren going full blast.

She mailed Olive's letter and hurried back. Since she was fully dressed, Allegra decided she might as well have breakfast in the dining room. Perhaps Olive, who had also dressed early, would like to join her. If so, Olive would have to be told before she ordered breakfast for two in their room.

All the old wives' tales about a brisk morning's walk whetting one's appetite were only too true. Today Allegra would love to have an English breakfast with a boiled egg and a rasher of bacon instead of the continental croissants and brioches. Not that they weren't served in England. You ate what you paid for—or, in this case, what Olive paid for.

In the last block, Allegra saw the back end of an automobile sticking out beyond the tunnel-like walls. It had something funny on top... why, it looked like the police car she had spied on her way to the post office! She quickened her already hurrying steps. The police car had stopped behind the Cité Hotel. Allegra hurried around the corner to see what was going on. Four or five men in uniform, porters, chambermaids, and kitchen staff from the hotel were all clustered about the back door and a row of oversize garbage cans. What in the world...?

Hunger forgotten, Allegra joined the peering knot, intent on the can where the uniformed men were thickest. One of them stepped back and she caught a glimpse of a woman's shoulder in a plaid jacket—crossing lines of red, yellow, green, brown... my God, Olive! Olive, who had been dressed and could have gone out while Allegra was at the post office. What was she wearing this morning? But she couldn't have been wearing that suit, Allegra thought. That was the one she'd wrecked at Nîmes, the one she gave to the chambermaid...

Another policeman moved and Allegra got a glimpse of light brown hair the color of Olive's. Her heart bumped again. But it couldn't be—it couldn't. A glimpse of a twisted neck, a three-quarter face... A face she'd never seen before.

Allegra shrank back, ashamed of the relief that poured through her. The poor woman! Oh, the poor woman! To think of someone...

"What—what happened to her? Was she murdered? How did—" Allegra stopped. The people around her were talking, but not in her language. The man beside her said something in French. She made the response that was now automatic, "*Je ne parle pas Français.*"

She tried again on her other side. "What happened, do you know?"

The man shrugged. He spoke in French, and she shrugged back. How maddening wanting to find out something when you didn't know how to ask the questions and wouldn't have understood the answers anyway. It had to be murder. Women who died natural deaths did not put themselves in garbage cans and pull the lid on over them.

Two policemen reached into the can and Allegra turned away, trying not to run. She couldn't stand and watch while they dragged that poor woman out, if that was what they were going to do. Even if they weren't, she'd had enough.

Shivering, fighting nausea, Allegra hurried around the corner to the front door of the hotel. The concierge would tell her... but the concierge wasn't at his desk. Even the telephone operator had vanished. The hotel simply wasn't doing business. She hoped this wouldn't be the moment when Olive's cable came through.

She hurried up to the second floor, stumbling up the stairs instead of waiting for the elevator. Her key wouldn't fit in the lock and as she was fumbling with it, Olive opened the door from the other side.

Allegra all but fell in.

"What in the world—? What's the matter, Allegra?" Olive asked. "You're white as a sheet and you're shaking. Are you sick?"

Olive led her to a chair and pushed her into it.

"My God, Olive, a woman's been killed and p-p-put into a garbage can—and she had on your suit," Allegra stammered.

"Who? What woman, Allegra?" Olive said. "What do you mean 'had on my suit?'"

"Well, the jacket anyway," Allegra said. "That's all I could see without getting any closer, but I didn't want to."

Olive shook her arm in exasperation.

"Who?" she demanded. "What woman are you talking about? Pull yourself together, Allegra."

"I don't know who she is," Allegra said. "I never saw her before. She was wearing the suit you gave the chambermaid. The one you wrecked in Nîmes."

"You're sure it wasn't the chambermaid I gave it to?" Olive said. "Maybe you didn't recognize her."

"I know it wasn't that chambermaid," Allegra assured her. "This woman was much younger and not nearly so dark. Her hair color was similar to yours, and with that suit on—my God, Olive, for a minute I thought it was you."

Olive absently patted the arm she had shaken.

"Then I remembered you'd given that suit away," Allegra added.

"Have you told the concierge?" Olive asked. "I suppose the police have been called. How did you discover this—body anyway?"

"The back of the hotel is crawling with police," Allegra said. "That's what made me go there. Most of the hotel staff's out there too. Olive… it came to me… since she's wearing your suit, you don't suppose we'll be involved, do you?"

"As I said before, Allegra, pull yourself together," Olive said. "How could we be involved? If you've never seen the woman before, I'm sure I haven't either. And she wasn't even the woman I gave the suit to. Maybe we'll be questioned to prove the suit wasn't stolen. If things get too sticky for Brian to handle, I'll send for Foster McKane. What's a lawyer for if not to get you, or keep you, out of trouble? Heaven knows, I pay him enough."

"Can he drop everything and come, just like that?" Allegra asked.

"If he wants to keep my business he will." Olive's tone indicated she would put up with no nonsense. "Besides, he's got partners to keep things going. I wonder if there's any use trying to order breakfast or if the whole staff's still out there gawking."

"I'm not hungry," Allegra said weakly.

"Well, I am," Olive said. "I got up early to write that letter. Funny, if I should have to send for Foster, he won't even get it."

It was a good half hour before Olive was able to put in her order and nearly another before the rolls and coffee arrived. By then Allegra was able to nibble at a croissant, and she drank her hot coffee gratefully. She had just shaken out the last drops from the little pot when the first knock came at the door.

It was Winifred, bright-eyed with what she thought would be titillating news.

"You'll never believe it," she burst out. "There's been a murder in our hotel!"

"Do you know who that woman was?" Olive asked.

"Do I—?" Winifred deflated. "You mean you've already heard?"

"I went out early and saw the police…" Allegra shivered again.

Jen appeared in the open doorway, glasses and hair awry. She looked at the three women and straightened her glasses.

"I guess Winifred's told you about the latest excitement," she said.

"Yes." Allegra nodded. "Do you know who the woman is?"

Neither visitor did.

"It's so hard to understand what they tell you," Winifred said. "But Brian will know. I saw him down there."

"She was wearing your suit, Olive!" Jen cried. "That lovely plaid you bought in Scotland and had made up."

"Oh, yes," Winifred said. "I couldn't believe my eyes. You'd better check your clothes, Olive. Someone must be stealing them."

"I gave that suit to one of the chambermaids," Olive told them. "It got wrecked in that fall in Nîmes."

"That's good," Winifred said, "because I'm sure you wouldn't want it now. There's a big slit in the back where the knife—"

"Winifred, don't!" Allegra cried.

"I don't think she was one of the chambermaids," Jen said. "At least I've never seen her around the hotel." She began to twist her hair.

"No wonder your hair never stays in place, Jen." Winifred was willing to turn her attention to lesser matters than murder. "You keep fiddling with it all the time."

Jen pushed up her glasses. "Sorry, it's a habit I have when I'm nervous."

"It's one you ought to make yourself get over," Winifred said. "You can always—"

"Here's Brian," Olive interrupted. "Now we can get some information."

He came through the open door. "What don't you know? With both Winifred and Jen here, you can't have missed much."

"Who was she, Brian?" Allegra asked. "Why was the poor woman killed? Who—?"

"One at a time, friend, one at a time," Brian said. "She was a girl from the new town. All the staff knew her. Her name was Marie Girard. I got the impression there was something crooked going on between her and one or two of the chambermaids here, but no one really said anything definite. That's the sort of thing that filters out later and there might be some connection—" He interrupted himself. "Olive, did you know that Marie Girard had on one of your suits?"

"Winifred and, Jen and Allegra all told me," Olive said. "It was the suit I was wearing when I fell in the Nîmes Colosseum, and I'd have had to have large hunks of it rewoven or give it away. So I gave it to one of the chambermaids. The other woman must have gotten it from her."

"It gave me an awful shock at first," Allegra said. "I couldn't see her face and I thought it was Olive till I remembered she'd given that suit away."

"I know what you mean," Jen sympathized. "I saw her face first, so I knew it wasn't Olive, yet my eyes kept going back to that suit. It gave me the creeps."

"I saw the suit before I saw the face," Winifred said. "Only I didn't know Olive had given it away."

"Carry on, girls." Brian's smile touched each woman separately. "It wasn't Olive in the suit. And whatever shock you got is past history now. I don't think the police will question any of us since the girl didn't work here, unless they routinely ask all the guests whether they've ever seen her around the hotel. And they might want to verify your giving away the suit, Olive."

"But she wasn't the one I gave it to," Olive said.

"If the skullduggery going on here that the police hinted at had anything to do with clothing—and I got the impression it did—they'll need to confirm that bit about the suit," Brian said. "Probably the concierge will come with them to make sure the guests are treated tenderly and to act as interpreter if needed, but if you have any problem at all, shout for me. I'm thinking particularly about you, Olive. But the offer holds good for all of you."

Again, Brian's smile touched each of them.

"We'll get more information about the murder and the victim as the day goes on," he continued. "I'll go back now and see what else I can pick up."

"Are we going to Narbonne today, Brian?" Winifred asked.

"I think we'd better plan to stay here today," Brian said. "Since we're going to be here longer than we planned anyway, it won't interfere with our sightseeing and ought to make a better impression on the police. All the other tourists will be clamoring to get away. Anyone want to come with me now? Take care then. I'll let you know what I find out."

It was lunchtime before they saw Brian again. The hum of conversation in the dining room was louder than usual. Above it he asked, "Have the police been in yet?"

Olive shook her head.

"They will be," Brian assured them. "They do want you to identify the clothes and verify giving them away."

"I told you that was Olive's suit, Elmer," Cicely announced triumphantly.

Margot leaned forward with her young sweep of hair.

"I was sure of it," she said. "How did that woman get it, Olive? You didn't know her, did you?"

Olive told her story about the suit again, ending, "I suppose the chambermaid gave it to the woman who was killed."

"What did you find out, Brian, about—" Allegra paused "—that woman and what happened this morning?"

"She and one of the chambermaids here were working some kind of racket in stolen nylons," Brian explained. "It was certainly a very minor racket—the chambermaid apparently stole a new pair of stockings out of the tourists' luggage, not more than one pair per bag so it wouldn't be noticed. She'd wrap them up and put them in an empty garbage can for the other woman to pick up."

"Have they found out where the knife came from, Brian?" Cicely asked.

"No, but I think they'll have a problem there," he said. "It was one of those knives made for the tourist trade that you find all over France, all over Europe, for that matter."

"Making it for the tourist trade doesn't mean a tourist had to buy it," Elmer remarked. "Local money's as good as tourist money."

"And a local customer'd probably get it cheaper," Winifred said.

"I don't know what there is that's so repulsively fascinating about a murder," Olive admitted. "I'm going to hate finding out and yet I want to know how it was done. We can't read the harrowing details in the newspaper here; it's all in French."

"The police say she was apparently bending over to take the package out of the can," Brian told her, "when someone came up from behind, stabbed her, and dumped her body into the can, using the momentum already started by her bending, to get the body inside fast."

"In other words, it wouldn't take an awful lot of strength, like picking her up from the ground," Margot amplified.

"In still other words," Elmer said, "the killer could be a woman as well as a man."

"The local women are nearly as muscular as men, anyway, I've noticed," Brian said.

"Oh, you've noticed?" Cicely stifled a giggle.

"What time was she killed, Brian? Did you find out?" Jen asked.

"A rough guess, from the condition of the body and the last time the kitchen staff dumped garbage, puts it at somewhere between six and seven this morning," Brian said.

"What about fingerprints on the knife?" Cicely asked. "Or maybe on the garbage can? If the murderer put the lid on..."

"They probably wore gloves," Winifred said. "They always do in books."

"Maybe the killers of Carcassonne don't read books," Brian said. "The hilt of the knife is too rough for fingerprints. Of course, they might get something off the can... what I can't figure out is *why* she was killed. She sold the nylons the chambermaid stole, but at one pair per tourist bag, that was only a pin-money racket. She couldn't have been killed for that."

"Still, it is money, and what looks small to a tourist might not look small to a local Frenchman," Elmer said.

"She was young and sort of attractive. I suppose there could be a sex angle," Cicely suggested.

Elmer grinned. "You would think of a sex angle."

"These impulsive Latin lovers." Margot looked at Henri, too far away at his isolated table to hear what was being said at Olive's table.

The others, too, looked at Henri. But their glances were kind, Allegra thought; everybody liked him.

"There'll be more coming out," Brian said. "I'll keep an ear to the ground."

"Your French ear," Allegra advised, remembering her own frustration behind the hotel.

"Revenge might be a motive," Jen mused.

Winifred said didactically, "I believe the two main motives for murder are money—including pin-money—and sex."

Olive had heard that word enough. She stood up; there would be no lingering for digestive conversation today.

"Come on, Allegra," she said. "If the police are on their way to see us, we'd better get to our room."

Allegra glanced back. At the table they had left, the heads moved closer. She saw Margot beckon to Henri. Now they'd order a bottle of wine, making sure it would not be put on Mrs. Wallace's account, and have a cozy chat about murder—probably murders in general, and certainly this murder in particular. Thank God it wasn't Olive. And she didn't need to feel guilty, she told herself; being glad one person hadn't been killed didn't mean she was glad another one had instead. Instead? What was she thinking of? Instead of Olive? Surely there was no question… Allegra remembered that ghastly second or two when she'd thought it as Olive. Her suit—

"Here are the police now," Olive said. "We made it back in time."

The concierge was standing in the hall with two men in uniform, and they all stepped aside politely while Allegra unlocked the door. Olive and Allegra preceded them inside.

One of the uniformed men walked over to the writing table and opened a package he was carrying, roughly wrapped in newspaper.

"Have you seen this—clothes before, Mesdames?" he asked.

"This is Madame Wallace," the concierge said. "And Madame Tate."

The policeman unfolded the suit Olive had given away, which had been wrapped in the newspaper, and held up the jacket.

"It was mine," Olive said. "I gave it to one of the chambermaids a few days ago."

The policeman looked so incredulous that Allegra added, "She had a fall in Nîmes and the suit was damaged. See, under the sleeve…"

The policeman held up one sleeve, then the other.

"Look, Olive," Allegra exclaimed, "she didn't reweave it, she sewed it together, but see how nicely it's done. You would hardly know it was mended."

"'She,' Madame?" the policeman said.

"I was thinking of the chambermaid Madame Wallace gave it to, but maybe it was the other woman, the one who was killed," Allegra said.

"You saw her, Madame?" the policeman said.

"Only her shoulder and part of her face." Allegra shuddered, remembering.

"Have you ever seen her before?" the policeman said.

Allegra said, "No," shaking her head.

The policeman turned to Olive. "And you, Madame?"

"I doubt it. I twisted my ankle in that fall when the suit was damaged in Nîmes—" Olive held out a foot on which the ankle was now only slightly swollen "—so I seldom get out of the hotel. I didn't see her—the body—so I don't really know what she looked like."

The other policeman pulled two photographs out of a big envelope he was carrying, and both women looked at them. They were front and profile views of the woman Allegra had seen crumpled up in the big garbage can, taken, she thought shivering again, after death.

Olive shook her head. "No, I've never seen her."

"Not around the hotel?"

She shook her head again. "Not any place," she said firmly.

"Do you know the name of the chambermaid you give this—clothes to, Madame?" the policeman asked.

"I have no idea." Olive turned to the concierge. "She was that dark, middle-aged woman with heavy black brows that almost meet above her nose—the one you sent to my room when Mister Gifford told you I had some things that needed cleaning. The day after we arrived..."

"Oh, yes." The concierge spattered French at the policeman who had been doing the talking.

He turned back to Olive. "What day was that Madame, when you give this—clothes to the maid?"

"The day after we arrived," Olive repeated. "Let's see... was that last Monday, Allegra?"

"We got here Monday, so it was Tuesday the chambermaid came, and you gave her the suit," Allegra told her.

The concierge nodded his confirmation. "That was the day I sent her to see you. *Mardi...*" He was talking in French again with both the policemen this time.

"Does this maid take care of your room?" the one who spoke English asked.

"No." Olive had been shaking her head enough today to make her dizzy, Allegra thought hysterically. "Our chambermaid is that thin old lady with almost white hair." Olive looked toward the concierge for verification.

"*Oui, oui,* yes," he agreed.

The policeman who spoke English looked at Allegra.

"How is it that you see the body this morning, Madame?" he said. "Madame Wallace says she did not."

"I went out early to mail a letter," Allegra said. "Earlier than usual for me. I usually don't get out before ten."

"How early was that Madame?" the policeman asked.

"A little after eight," Allegra said.

"Where were you between six and seven, Madame?"

"This morning?" Allegra said. "I was in bed, sound asleep. I nearly always sleep late because I don't sleep well the early part of the night."

"And you, Madame?" the policeman asked Olive.

"I wasn't asleep, but I can assure you I didn't leave this room," Olive said, a note of indignation in her voice.

The concierge began to talk rapidly in French. By his earnest air, by tone and gesture, he seemed to be objecting to something.

The policeman who had unwrapped Olive's suit folded it again and wrapped it in the newspaper, bowed formally, and marched to the door. The second policeman bowed and followed.

"I am so sorry, Madame," the concierge said, looking distressed. "*Les gendarmes*—please do not think they suspect you—of anything. It is just the way of the police. They think they have to ask these questions of everybody, even the most respected, upright, honored..." He ran out of English adjectives, bowed twice, once to each lady, and murmured, "Do not take offense, I beg you," as he quickly followed the *gendarmes.*

"Allegra!" Olive was now highly indignant. "Don't tell me those policemen think I killed that girl to get my suit back!"

"Now that it's been so neatly mended?" Allegra said. "I don't think you need to worry, Olive. I think what the concierge said was right, that the police ask everybody these questions. And, after all, we were close enough to where it happened to nip out, as Brian would say, do the dirty work, and whip back in again with a good chance that no one would see us."

"Everybody in the hotel had the opportunity," Olive said. "But what about motive? Motive and opportunity are supposed to be so important, and I simply can't imagine any guest in this hotel being motivated to kill a local woman. Can you?"

"There are possible reasons, Olive," Allegra said. "Suppose this girl had something on one of the guests and was blackmailing him—"

"How could she possibly know enough about a guest to blackmail him?" Olive asked.

"I didn't say probable. I said possible..." Allegra said. Into her mind came a picture of Brian softly closing Winifred's door at two in the morning, the sound of his voice coming from Jen's room after midnight. If someone knew of Olive's feeling about sex (and all of her tour guests did), the threat of three more names being dropped from her will... any of the three would be willing to pay to keep her from knowing. A hotel employee might well be in a position to—

"Nonsense!" Olive's voice broke into her thoughts as if she could read them.

Allegra blinked. "What's nonsense?"

"Where's your mind, Allegra?" Olive asked. "We were talking about the possibility of a local woman blackmailing one of the hotel guests."

Olive didn't know what Allegra knew, but the possibility of a local woman's knowing was even more remote.

"If it was someone in the hotel," Allegra mused, "it seems to me it would be much more likely to be one of the staff members than one of the guests."

"That's a happy thought," Olive said. "Maybe our beds are being made by a murderer."

"That thin little old lady?" Allegra said.

"Maybe it's that pink-cheeked boy who usually brings our breakfast trays," Olive said. "Does that make you feel any more comfortable?"

Allegra laughed and shivered at the same time. "Murder doesn't make for comfortable feelings."

"I don't like that policeman's attitude," Olive said, "and I'd certainly be interested in knowing whether he asks the other hotel guests where they were between six and seven this morning."

"Don't take it so personally, Olive," Allegra said. "I'm sure it would be a standard question, and that's probably why the concierge went along—to reassure the others as he did us. The hotel's business depends on tourists. He'd want to make sure they weren't offended. We can hardly canvass the whole hotel, but we can certainly find out from our group what he asked them."

Olive was ready to start but Allegra stopped her.

"We have to give the police time to see them first—all of them," Allegra said. "How's it going to look if we slide right into each room as soon as the police leave it?"

"Maybe a little too interested," Olive admitted.

At the end of a toe-tapping hour, Allegra gave in, and they went next door to see Jen. She looked as excited as she had the day Allegra bumped into her coming out of Brian's room, but there was none of that triumphant look in her face this time.

Jen got her question in first. "Did the police come to see you? They've just been here."

Simultaneously Allegra said, "Yes," and Olive said, "What did they ask you?"

"They wanted to know whether I'd ever seen the woman who was killed before I saw her—out there," Jen said.

"Had you?" Allegra asked.

Jen shook her head. "They said, she didn't work in the hotel, and certainly I've never seen her here, or on the street either. And they asked me if I'd ever seen the clothes she was wearing. Well, I had indeed, but on you, Olive, not her. They wanted to know if I knew you'd given them away. But I don't think any of us did, unless you did, Allegra."

"I was there when she gave them away," Allegra conceded.

"They seem determined to think she stole that suit," Olive said. "And maybe she did, but not from me."

"Which one of the chambermaids did you give it to, Olive," Jen asked, "that old lady who does our rooms?"

"No, it was someone the concierge sent from downstairs—a dark, middle-aged woman with heavy black eyebrows," Olive said. "I've only seen her once or twice, and always on the ground floor."

"Handy to the garbage can," Winifred commented. They hadn't noticed her come in through the open door.

"Did the police come to your room, Winifred?" Allegra asked.

"They certainly did, but they didn't stay long," she said. "They asked a few questions and left."

"What questions?" Olive asked.

Winifred went through the same list Jen had, with one addition. "Do you know," Winifred exclaimed indignantly, "they actually had the nerve to ask me where I was between six and seven this morning? As if they thought I might have killed that girl!"

"They asked me that too," Jen said. "I supposed it was routine. Good heavens, you don't think they thought—?"

She broke off, looking upset.

"That's what Olive was worried about too," Allegra said. "But I told her I was sure it was something they'd ask everyone."

There were voices in the hall and, as one woman, all four made for the door. The police and the concierge were leaving the Andersons' room.

As the three men walked down the hall, Margot's door opened. She turned toward the Andersons' room and saw the four women across the hall. Cicely saw them too and called to Elmer, who had gone back inside, and all seven met in the hall.

"Isn't this exciting?" Cicely's face was lighted up and her eyes sparkled.

"Too exciting," Olive said flatly. "Did they ask you where you were between six and seven, Elmer?"

"They sure did, and—" Elmer began.

"And Elmer couldn't tell them," his wife interrupted, giggling. "This ought to teach him to stay in bed in the morning like normal people. Now I could say in all honesty that I hadn't been outside our room."

"You had dressed and gone out, Elmer?" Olive asked.

"Unfortunately, yes," he said. "I can't sleep late, so I usually go for a walk before breakfast."

Winifred said she always took a walk before breakfast. Jen said she sometimes did, and, like Elmer, this had unfortunately been one of those mornings.

"There must have been something in the air," Margot said. "I practically always sleep late, but this morning I woke up early, and the sun was so beautiful I couldn't stay in bed."

"Brian and Henri were out too," Winifred said. "Henri was working on the car and Brian was talking to him when I left the hotel about six-thirty."

"Looks like most of you were out roaming the streets at the time of the murder," Olive said slowly. "I wonder what the police make of that?"

"They won't make anything of it," Elmer said. "You'd be surprised how many tourists take morning constitutionals. I even saw one fellow jogging."

"They asked us all where we were between six and seven," Olive persisted. "Cicely and Allegra and I were the only ones who weren't fully dressed and out of doors where we could have—" She stopped.

"Forget it, Olive." Elmer patted her shoulder reassuringly. "The police are going to require a lot more than that before they risk arresting a tourist. Anyway, how could they possibly tie up one of us with a local resident involved in penny-ante black-market shenanigans?"

"I wonder if the other hotel guests were asked that question," Olive mused, "or if it's specifically us they're suspicious of."

"They're not suspicious of us," Elmer said, patting her shoulder again. "I'm sure it's a routine question. But I'll check around the people I know here and find out what they've been asked."

Margot and the Andersons went downstairs, while the four others returned to their rooms.

Inside, Olive turned to Allegra.

"What in the world is the matter?" she said. "Ever since we found out that you and I and Elmer's wife were the only ones who weren't outdoors at the time of the murder, you haven't said a word, not a peep. And you've been looking downright sick. What is it? What are you thinking?"

Allegra reached for the nearest chair.

"I put one set of facts with another set of facts and they—they add up," Allegra said. "My God, how they add up!"

"Allegra! What on earth—?" Olive began.

"We've found out that Elmer and Brian and Henri and Jen and Winifred and Margot all had an opportunity to kill that woman—near the place where she was killed at the time she was killed."

"But why would they want to kill an unknown French woman?" Olive asked.

"What if they didn't know she was an *unknown* French woman?" Allegra said. "If they only saw her from the back... she was wearing your suit and had hair the same color as yours."

"Allegra, you don't mean—you can't mean—" Olive said.

"Yes, I do," Allegra said. "None of them knew you'd given that suit away. Whoever stabbed that woman may have thought it was you."

Olive swallowed hard. "But surely no one on the hotel staff—"

"It didn't have to be one of the hotel staff," Allegra said. "It could have been Elmer or Brian or Henri or Jen or Winifred or Margot. And if it was, they did it because they thought it was you."

It was Olive who reached for a chair now.

"My God, Allegra..." she began.

"It could have been," Allegra said.

Olive swallowed again. "Now I *am* going to send for my lawyer."

Chapter Sixteen

The call to Foster McKane was one Olive preferred to make herself. Allegra could hear her talking to the operator, to the concierge, to the operator, and then to the concierge again. Allegra knew when she got the United States because the concierge was left out of the conversation. At last Allegra heard her say, "Hello, hello, Foster!"

Allegra turned off the listening part of her mind. She had other things to think about, primarily one other thing. Should she say anything to the police about the possibility of mistaken identity? If she did, she'd have to go into her fears for Olive, the will, and the accidents. Would the French policeman's understanding of English be equal to all that? She couldn't call on Brian's services as interpreter. He was one of the chief suspects—in fact, her chief suspect. She'd have to appeal to the concierge. Now, why did it seem so much worse to tell all this to one of the hotel staff than to a policeman? But it did. They were all guests here on an equal footing. If everyone but Allegra and Olive and Cicely were suspects, how would he feel about the rest of his guests? He'd want to protect them, but would that...?

She was being idiotic. But at least she had demonstrated that if she told her story to any Frenchman, it would have to be to the police. If they believed her, they'd never let the tour go on—in fact, they might be stuck in Carcassonne for the rest of the summer. Think of all the reservation cancellations that would involve!

Allegra switched her mind back to the telephone and to Olive's conversation. Foster McKane spoke French. He'd had a couple of years at the Sorbonne and married a French girl he'd met there. Maybe Olive should ask her to come too. Money was no object...

At the moment, Olive was only listening. Then she said, "But, Foster, you've got to come. I need you. I tell you, my life's in danger!"

If that didn't get him, what would? Olive must be his best client, unless some corporation beat her out.

"Fly to Paris," Olive insisted, "and then take a plane to Toulouse. We'll meet you there with the motor coach."

Did that mean he was coming? Allegra found herself praying: *Dear God, please make Foster come. This is something I can't cope with.*

"You could be here tomorrow, or at least the next day," Olive pleaded. "But I need you now. Please try to make it by tomorrow."

Olive, saying please.

She gave a long sigh. "Oh, thank you, Foster. If you need to reach me, don't cable, telephone. Unless I get a call to the contrary, I'll check what time your plane's due from Paris and meet you in Toulouse. If there's no connection, I'll charter a plane and leave word at the Pan-Am desk, so be sure to check there. I can't tell you how much I appreciate this and how relieved I feel. I'm really grateful, Foster."

Olive, making a production of gratitude.

She couldn't be any more grateful than Allegra. The two women sat looking at each other, visibly relaxing.

"He'll try to get a plane to Paris tonight and catch one to Toulouse tomorrow," Olive explained. "If it turns out to be one of those once-a-week flights and there's no charter available, I'll die."

"Don't say that Olive," Allegra said.

Olive tried to smile.

Now Allegra could transfer her latest problem to Foster McKane. He'd know whether the police should be told about her speculations.

Meanwhile, she had to help Olive stay alive until he got there.

Chapter Seventeen

"There's one thing we've got to be careful about—no, two," Allegra corrected herself. "It goes without saying that you mustn't be physically in any dangerous position, Olive, like being alone in your room with any of your guests, not even Margot or Jen or Winifred. A woman could have killed that Marie What's-her-name. And you certainly mustn't stand by the edge of the wall on the terrace, or any other drop-off. The other thing is, we mustn't say or do anything that would lead anyone to think—and I do mean anyone—that the idea of that girl being mistaken for you has entered our heads."

Olive shuddered. "It's hardly anything I'd choose for a topic of conversation."

"In case there is something to that theory, we don't want even a hint to get out until we can tell Foster McKane and he can discuss it with the police if he decides it's the thing to do," Allegra said. "Thank God he speaks French. And I'll ask a few questions before he gets here."

"You'll ask questions?" Olive asked.

"I thought I'd do a little checking on these early morning strolls our friends have been taking—where they went—who they saw—that kind of thing," Allegra explained.

"Good heavens, Allegra, do you think that's being careful?" Olive said. "If they think you're suspicious—"

"They won't," Allegra assured her. "I won't ask that kind of question. They'll just think I'm a nosy old gal, which God knows I am, taking a morbid interest in murder."

119

Olive was looking worried again. "I wish you wouldn't," she said. "You might give away our suspicions without meaning to and besides—"

"Besides what?" Allegra asked.

"I'm afraid," Olive admitted. "I've been afraid something might happen to me for a long time now. I don't want to be afraid something's going to happen to you, too. Allegra, I want to tell you while I still can that I appreciate all the support you've given me. There's no one else I could have turned to not knowing..."

Olive paused and leaned against her bed.

"There's another thing I think you ought to know, though it's hard to tell you," she continued. "The reason I'm not leaving you any money isn't because of anything you've done or haven't done. You're not like Jen, who does all right at her job, but is so utterly helpless at living. It's because of Bob."

"Bob!" Allegra exclaimed.

"You and Bob were so happy, I was plain envious," Olive said. "It seemed to me you had everything—love, happiness, even a baby. And all I had was money; not that I wanted Bob, but I wanted what you had, and I suppose I never forgave you for having it when I didn't."

"Olive, my dear," Allegra began. To Allegra's horror, her voice broke. She put a hand on the other woman's arm.

Olive shook it off.

"Let's not get sentimental," she said. "There's always something behind the way people act and I thought you ought to know why I've been so—bitchy, I think's the word you'd use."

Allegra gave a shaky little laugh. In her experience, such a word had never passed Olive's lips before.

Someone knocked on the door and both women jumped.

Allegra opened it, and the Andersons came in.

"I wanted to put your mind at rest right away, Olive," Elmer said. "I talked to half a dozen other people at this hotel and every one of them said the police asked them where they were between six and seven this morning. So you see, you didn't need to worry. I was sure it was simply routine."

"Thank you, Elmer," Olive said. "That was thoughtful of you."

"When you were out this morning, Elmer," Allegra said, "did you see anyone near the back of the hotel?"

"I've been trying to recall that very thing, Allegra," he said. "I was out at the time the murder was supposed to have happened, and we all have to pass by that way to get out of the square. Of course, you can't actually see the garbage cans from the street, and I saw quite a number of people while I was out, but I don't remember seeing any locals near the back of the hotel, or even any tourists except Henri, who was working on the bus with his head hidden by the hood and paying no attention to anything but his work. That young fellow's a good worker."

"Isn't he?" Allegra agreed. "He seems like a nice person too."

"You know, the next time I go on a trip I'm going to bring a camera," Elmer said. "There's a fellow, I think he's staying at the other hotel—you never see him without a camera. He says if he doesn't have a big one hanging around his neck, he always has a little candid type with him. He claims his pictures may not be as good as a professional's but they mean a lot more to him because he always gets people in them even if it's some fat lady climbing into a tour bus. I've always thought cameras were a nuisance but, what the hell, I've got so much to carry anyway."

He glanced at his wife and added, "Think of the views I could get of you, honey."

"Elmer! What do you mean by that?" Cicely cuddled up against him like a kitten, and they left with his arm around her waist.

"You see," Allegra said, "he wasn't upset when I asked if he'd seen anyone near the back of the hotel."

"Well, you did ask it casually and sort of naturally," Olive said.

"That's the way I'd be with everybody," Allegra said. "I don't want to upset the apple cart any more than you do."

The next person Allegra saw was Jen, who came by to ask if she and Olive wanted to walk down to the fruit stands with her.

Allegra reached promptly for her handbag, wishing she could think of some way to remind Olive, without saying the words aloud, not to let anyone in while she was gone.

"Why don't you take a rest, Olive?" Allegra said. "You've had a trying day. I'll leave the door locked and if anyone knocks, don't get up. They'll come back if it's important." She could only hope that Olive got the message.

"It really has been a trying day," Jen said as they walked down the hall. "Even if we didn't know that girl, something like that is extremely shocking."

And even more shocking, thought Allegra, if you thought that the knife was intended for the back of someone you knew.

They stepped out of the hotel into the late afternoon sunshine, but the high walls of the cathedral square cut off so much of it that only their motor coach—and Henri standing beside it washing it off with a hose—were in the sunshine. Beyond it, in the shadows, were two other larger tourist buses and several private cars.

"There're a lot of tourists in town," Jen said. "Funny how you can always tell them from the local people."

"Did you see many when you were out this morning?" Allegra asked.

"Many what—tourists or local people?" Jen asked.

"Either one," Allegra said. They were passing the end of the hotel, and it was around that corner...

Both women turned their heads away.

"Specifically," Allegra added, "did you see anyone around here?"

"I saw Henri at the bus as I was coming back but not on the way out, and I saw a couple of tourists," Jen said. "One of them was that jogger Elmer mentioned—about halfway down the block. And I saw a man who looked like a workman."

"Was he close to the back of the hotel?" Allegra asked.

"Not far, a little way down the street, going in the same direction I was, away from the hotel. He was walking fast and passed me," Jen said.

"How was he dressed?" Allegra asked.

"I don't know," Jen said. "You don't pay attention to that sort of thing when you're out for a walk. My impression was he had on dark clothes, but that's only a vague impression. I really have no idea what he wore."

"Was there anything special about the way he looked?" Allegra asked. "Do you think you'd recognize him if you saw him again?"

"I'm sure I wouldn't," Jen said. "I didn't even look at his face, so there'd be no use showing me mug shots. Or do the French police even do that sort of thing? You know how it is, Allegra, you get a vague impression of a local workman and actually, he may not have been that at all."

"You said he was walking fast?" Allegra said.

"Fast enough to pass me, and I wasn't sauntering," Jen said. "That's not how you take a morning constitutional, as Elmer calls it."

"Did he give you the feeling he was running away from something?" Allegra said.

"Didn't enter my head," Jen said.

"Or acting furtive in any way?" Allegra said.

"How do you act furtive, Allegra?" Jen asked. "He was walking fast, that's all I can say."

"Have you told the police?" Allegra asked.

"What's there to tell them?" Jen said. "I couldn't possibly identify the man. I couldn't even identify his walk. There was nothing distinctive about it. He was simply walking faster than average."

All the rest of the way to the fruit stands, Allegra tried to pin Jen down, to get something definite from her. The fact that she had seen a man and that he had passed her at a fast walk were the only definite statements she was willing to make.

Allegra dropped the information into her mental storehouse for Foster McKane. She would let him decide whether the French police should know.

On the way back, Jen stopped at the little shop near the hotel where Cicely had seen the "groovy postcards."

In the hope that Henri would still be grooming the motor coach, Allegra increased her speed. At least now she wouldn't have to explain to Jen how she was suddenly able to talk with him. Too bad she couldn't get over feeling guilty about not telling Olive.

Henri was still there, polishing now instead of hosing. He smiled at Allegra, that charming, magnetic smile.

She walked around him to where she could keep an eye on the street leading out of the square and the door of the hotel at the same time. If it should be necessary to switch from English to animated shrugging and groping for one of her few French words, she would be warned in time.

"Wasn't it terrible about that poor girl this morning?" Allegra said. Since Henri was still being served at his segregated table, Allegra hadn't talked with him at lunch.

"*Oui, très mal.*" Henri shook his head and polished harder.

She'd better not waste time in preliminaries; someone they both knew might come along.

"I suppose the police—the *gendarmes*—talked with you?" Allegra asked.

He nodded, and his handsome brows drew together. His may have been a rougher interview than hers. The tour group was foreign and had to get the kid-glove treatment, but Henri was French and didn't.

"What time did you come outdoors, Henri?" Allegra said.

"About *six heure quinze*—seex feefteen, Madame," he said. "I thought we were going to Narbonne, and the motor needed some work. Since we did not go, I could have slept."

"Did you see anyone go around the corner at the back of the hotel?" Allegra asked.

"*Non,* Madame," Henri assured her. "*Les gendarmes* ask me that too. I see nobody, not even the friends of Madame Wallace until Brian stop to talk with me. As soon as I come out of the hotel, my face it is—how you say?—buried in the motor. The bonnet is up, I see nothing but the motor. I tell *les gendarmes* that is all I see."

Judging by his expression, he must have had a hard time convincing the police that he was telling the truth. How could she hope to get any more information from him than they had? But she tried once more. "You didn't see Mademoiselle Cooper or Mademoiselle Jenkins, or Brian till he spoke to you. Not even Mademoiselle Scott?"

"He saw Mademoiselle Scott," a voice behind her spoke.

Allegra jumped. Margot was standing right beside her.

"I told him it was okay to admit he saw me," Margot said. "If he didn't, Brian would. I was talking to Henri when Brian came along."

Margot's brown eyes were fixed steadily on Allegra, who asked, "Did you notice where Brian came from?"

Margot shook her head. "I was talking to Henri, and I always look at the person I'm talking to, when suddenly there was Brian."

"What time was it when you came out, Margot?" Allegra asked.

"I didn't notice," Margot said. "The sunlight woke me, and I got up to close the curtains so I could go back to sleep, and I saw Henri out the window working on the car. I thought I'd get dressed and talk to him while he worked."

"After Brian came, did you stay and talk to him too or go back to your room?" Allegra asked.

"Neither," Margot said. "The morning was so lovely and fresh and bright that I went for a little walk myself—down as far as the post office and then up that hill past the Donjon Hotel. Isn't that a neat name for a hotel?"

For once, Allegra wasn't distracted into irrelevant discussion.

"Did you see anyone besides Henri and Brian?" she asked.

"Quite a few people," Margot said. "I was amazed at how many get up so early, but I only saw one or two I knew. I saw Winifred off in the dim distance striding along and I saw Elmer's friend—the one who's always draped with cameras. I should think the sight of all that hardware would turn Elmer off instead of on. I followed the camera nut for about a block, and he was squirming and readjusting the load and fiddling with it most of the way. He must have either finished taking some pictures or was getting ready to. You couldn't pay me to go to all that bother."

"Me neither," Allegra agreed absently. "Did you see anyone near the back of the hotel?"

"The scene of the crime?" Margot said. "The camera nut was the closest one, and he was halfway down that first block when I saw him. Besides, I really think he was too loaded down to have stuck a knife into anyone, and he'd have probably dropped a camera in the garbage can when he pushed her in."

Allegra couldn't help laughing.

"I think we can rule him out," she agreed. "You don't remember anyone else?"

"I saw Jen staring up at the chateau in a trance on my way back, and a few

125

minutes later I saw Elmer talking to his camera friend down one of the little narrow side streets. I can't think of anyone else that I'd ever seen before," Margot said.

"If you should, will you let me know?" Allegra said. "It might be useful. Oh, there's Brian. I want to catch him. Thank you both for bearing with me."

Brian had come out of the arched doorway of the hotel as they were talking, raised a greeting hand, and started up the street.

Allegra hurried after him. "Brian!" she called.

He turned around and waited for her.

"Have you picked up anything new about the murder? At lunch you said—" Allegra said.

"I've kept my ear to the ground so long it's chafed," he told her, "and all I've been able to come up with is a little more on the girl's private life. It seems she was pretty widely disliked as a tramp and general troublemaker. There was even some hassle over a wedding that didn't come off. When she was a kid, her parents had arranged with the parents of the boy on an adjoining farm that the two would be married and the land thrown together. There may even have been a contract—"

"Brian," Allegra interrupted, "we're getting on toward the twenty-first century."

"Not a lot of the peasants around here," Brian said. "And I do mean peasants. The people I'm talking about are still on the farm. Probably the girl got tired of farm life and skipped out—to Carcassonne, the big city of the region. Anyway, the reports that got back to the farm were too much for the young man. He probably didn't like her anyway, so he eloped with someone else. They must have been living in this century."

"But if anyone was going to get killed because of that, wouldn't it have been the young man?" Allegra asked.

"That's what I'd think, and perhaps the police think so too because I understand they're still leaning toward the stocking-racket theory," Brian said. "If I were directing the investigation, I'd bear down harder on the tramp angle. There's nothing that hits a fellow where he lives like finding his girl's been two-timing him."

"You didn't see anyone yourself around the back of the hotel, did you, Brian?" Allegra said.

"This morning between six and seven?" Brian's usually pleasant smile turned down at the corners and his eyes weren't smiling at all.

"Of course between six and seven." Allegra decided to take the smile at, quite literally, face value. She smiled too. "Someone said, they saw a local workman or someone who looked like a local workman near there at that time. I wondered if you'd seen him."

"Who said that?" Brian asked. His smile was gone now, the question almost a bark.

"Why I—I don't remember," Allegra said. She wasn't going to give Jen away. It was Jen who had told her, wasn't it? Or could it have been Margot? "I've talked with so many people," she finished lamely.

"What are you trying to do, Allegra? Play detective?" Brian asked.

"It—it seemed possible that since you were out here you might have seen someone like that French workman—or something that would help," Allegra said.

"My God, you'd think this was a show put on for the tourists, like a sound and light performance!" Brian said. "Well, this is murder, Allegra. The police are the ones to handle it. Don't mess in. This is strictly a French affair."

Allegra blinked. This was more than she'd bargained for.

"I—I guess you're right," she stammered. "See you later."

Brian went on up the street.

Allegra turned back toward the hotel. She walked slowly. What did that strong reaction from Brian mean? It could be genuine concern for the safety of one of Olive's friends who was, in a sense, in his care. After all, a woman had been murdered, as he had pointed out with considerable vigor. But if Allegra's theory was right, it wasn't she who was in danger, it was Olive. Maybe that was why he'd been so upset. He hadn't known the suit had been given away. Maybe it was Brian. Allegra slowed her racing mind. Then a thought hit her like a knife in the back. She might have no money herself and her will left what property she had to Bob Jr., but if her nosiness threatened the killer's safety...

It wasn't only money and wills that led to murder.

Allegra reached her room, still shaking. As she tried without success to fit her key in the lock, the door across the hall opened.

"Whatever is the matter?" Winifred's usually expressionless face had an avid look. "If I hadn't known you for two years, I'd think you were drunk!"

"I guess I'm nervous," Allegra said. "Brian said something a few minutes ago that sort of bothered me."

"What'd he say?" Winifred said.

"Oh, something about it being dangerous to ask people where they were between six and seven and who they saw—that sort of thing," Allegra said.

Winifred laughed. "Don't tell me he thinks *you'll* be the next victim."

Allegra's hand was still shaking as she tried for the keyhole again. "If I ask the wrong questions, or ask the wrong person the right questions, or something. I don't suppose you'd—"

Winifred laughed again but this time she didn't sound amused. "Look out! Maybe you're about to ask the wrong person the right question. But I don't have a guilty conscience. Go ahead. What do you want to know?"

"Since you said you were outside at least part of the time between six and seven, I wondered if you saw anyone near the back of the hotel?" Allegra asked.

"The bus is parked in that general area, and I think I told you I saw Henri working on the engine and Brian talking to him," Winifred said. "I don't think I saw anyone else I knew till I was a couple of blocks away and I saw Jen window shopping at that jewelry store where I got my tourmaline. She was so absorbed I don't think she saw me when I passed. At least she didn't speak. And I saw Elmer's back going up a side street; I think it was the next one over. That's all I can remember right now. But it's hard to bring back a complete picture and I may think of someone else later."

"Did you see anyone who looked like a local workman?" Allegra asked.

"Several at that hour, but I don't remember seeing one of them near the back of the hotel," Winifred said.

"Thanks, Winifred. If you think of anything else, let me know." Allegra had finally connected the key with the lock. She turned it and went inside.

Olive was sitting on the side of her bed, looking alarmed.

"Thank goodness it's you, Allegra," Olive said. "I could hear someone fumbling at the lock and I thought maybe they were trying to pick it. You don't look yourself at all. What's the matter now?"

"I don't feel myself either," Allegra said. She told Olive about the bits and pieces of information she had picked up, ending with Brian's warning.

"It's what I told you, Allegra," Olive said. "It doesn't pay to get too curious about a murder, or the killer may think he has to kill you to protect himself."

"But I only talked with the people in our own group," Allegra said. "If anyone tried to get at me, that would mean my theory was right about mistaking her for you in that suit."

Olive's next question was dry.

"Which would you rather be—right or alive?"

Chapter Eighteen

They were still talking about the murder at dinner. And theirs wasn't the only table where the buzz of speculation was as loud as it had been at lunch. Even tourists who had recently arrived were buzzing and asking the waiters and those at the next table questions.

The wine drinkers in Olive's party had no opportunity to sit around the table sampling Carcassonne vintages tonight. As soon as the after-dinner coffee had been swallowed, Olive rose and announced she'd like to take a hand in the bridge game tonight. She, Jen, Winifred, and Elmer were soon hard at it.

Allegra looked about halfheartedly to see if they could get up another table, but Cicely was hanging over her husband's chair, Brian was heading out the door, and Margot had already disappeared.

Allegra stepped restlessly out onto the terrace. It was dark beyond the wall, but a lovely warm evening for a walk. Maybe Cicely would go with her. After this afternoon, Allegra felt reluctant to go out alone at night.

Cicely looked up as Allegra came into the room and said, "It's a lovely evening. Let's walk down to see the chateau. The floodlights should be on by now."

Olive's eyebrows went up. "You haven't forgotten there was a murder this morning, have you, Allegra?"

"We'll stick to the main street, which is pretty well lighted," Allegra promised. "Besides, there're two of us and I've been going out late—really late, alone."

Allegra turned to Cicely's husband. "Don't you think it's all right, Elmer?"

"If you do, stick to the main street," he said. "These little towns are quite safe, and this one's lousy with tourists. You'll probably run into Brian, and you can annex him. Anyway, Olive, that knifing this morning was a local matter. It didn't have anything to do with the tourists."

Briefly Olive's eyes met Allegra's.

"Well, be careful," Olive said. "It's your lead, Jen."

"Isn't it lovely tonight?" Allegra said as she and Cicely stepped outside. "I felt as if I'd start climbing the walls if I stayed inside another minute."

"I learn quite a lot about bridge from watching Elmer play, but they'll still be at it when we get back and the chateau is terrific all lit up at night," Cicely said.

But they didn't get that far. As they reached the place where the street morphed into the square, a figure stepped out of the shadows between their motor coach and the wall. A man they didn't know...

"Madame," he began, addressing Allegra. Then he burst into an unbroken, vehement stream of French with gestures.

"But—" Allegra began.

The stream of French flowed on. In the streetlight the man's face had a strange, almost green cast on top of dark violence. Both arms flew about, not in a way that could be called arm-waving. His arms were violent, flung out like blows, his hands fists.

The two women shrank together. Unable to understand a word of what he said, the gestures and the expression of his face were unmistakable. His whole figure menaced. Threat filled the night. The balmy, cathedral-dominated square was a place of terror.

He raised his hand to his throat and made a choking sound. The hand came out toward Allegra. Rooted to the cobblestones, she shrank back farther.

Cicely cried out, "Oh, thank God, here comes Brian!"

The man's head snapped up, turned toward the street. He dived back into the shadows he had come from.

"Brian! Brian!" Cicely called frantically.

Brian, who had been strolling along, broke into a run.

All either woman could do was babble, "Brian, Brian, a man— he threatened—"

"Go back to the hotel!" Brian ordered over his shoulder. He sprinted toward the parked cars.

The man darted out of the shadows between the wall and coach, then ran into the entrance to the street, all but flying down it.

"Brian!" Cicely screamed. "The street! There he goes!"

By the time Brian also was tearing down the street, the man had turned a corner and was out of sight.

Involuntarily the two women started out after them, but Allegra caught Cicely's arm. "Brian's right. We'd better go into the hotel. After what happened—and what might have happened…"

"I guess you're right." Reluctantly, Cicely turned back too. "Let's go to the door and wait. Then, if we see the wrong man coming, we can duck inside. Aren't you dying to know if Brian caught him?"

Cicely seemed to have lost all her fear and was now agreeably excited, eyes sparkling in the lights from the hotel windows.

"You're wonderful," Allegra said. "I'm still scared to death. But I guess I can stand up long enough to wait for Brian. I doubt if he'll catch that man. He knows the town better than Brian. He may even live nearby or have friends he can drop in on suddenly."

In the square, the night seemed stagnant. On the other nights when Allegra had been out, there had been much more activity, people coming and going, a bustle of cars. But tonight, all the time that fierce man had spat French at them—and it had seemed like forever while his flexing hands kept getting closer—no one had come along until Brian did. And no one had come since. The two men had dashed down an empty street, and the street was still empty. Was it like this in the morning when murder had been committed?

It seemed interminably long before they heard footsteps. A man came in sight—one man. He came closer, and they saw it was Brian.

Leaving the shelter of the hotel doorway, both women hurried toward him.

Brian shook his head. "He got away. After he turned that corner, he disappeared. I ran up and down the street he turned into and the streets going off it, and even stopped to listen. Nothing. No sight. No sound. What did he say to you? He was talking sixty to the dozen when I came along."

"He certainly was," Cicely said, while Allegra added, "In French."

"You couldn't get any of it?" Brian pressed. "Not even a few words?"

Both shook their heads.

"It was too fast and too frightening," Allegra said.

"He seemed to be threatening Allegra," Cicely said. "We couldn't understand what he was saying. But the way he looked and the way his hands went—it was like he was itching to hit her or choke her…"

They were both shivering again.

"Had you ever seen him before?" Brian asked.

Both heads shook and Allegra said, "God forbid I ever see him again. But if I did, I don't think I'd recognize him. It's after dark, the street light's not too good, and his face was so—so emotional—probably distorted with emotion… unless I could see that same expression again… which I hope I never will."

"Would you say he was a young man?" Brian asked. "Middle-aged? Old? He certainly didn't run like an old man."

"Middle," Allegra said. "What would you say, Cicely? About fifty?"

"Something like that," Cicely agreed. "Maybe younger—forty, forty-five…"

"And his build?" Brian asked. "One of those stocky types? Thin? Fat? Tall? Short? I only caught a glimpse before he shot around the corner."

Cicely provided the answer. "Stocky, leaning toward thin but not slender. I kept thinking he looked too muscular for even two of us to manage if it came to a struggle. Do you think we should call the police?"

Brian hesitated. "What would you say to them? That some man you'd never seen before and wouldn't recognize if you saw again began to talk to you in a language you couldn't understand so you didn't know what he said though he looked threatening while he said it? He may have done a lot of arm-waving, but he didn't touch either one of you. He didn't grab at your handbags. What the hell do you have to tell the police?"

Inside the hotel, Elmer and Winifred were of the same opinion. Jen thought the police should be told of the event even though there was no useful information to give them.

It was Olive, as usual, who decided. "You really haven't anything to tell them, either one of you. I think the police would feel you were wasting their time. And they'd do worse than that to ours if they felt that international relations required the man to be identified and admonished. On the strength of what you've told us, it certainly couldn't be a jailing matter, and we might lose a whole month of our time. If I thought it had anything to do with the murder... although I don't see how it could."

"Maybe you're right, Olive," Jen said doubtfully, her face reflecting the struggle between her own inclinations and her perpetual wish to agree with Olive. "You're so smart and you usually—you always seem to know what's the best thing to do."

Brian gave Cicely an untactful grin. "Brava, Jen, a very neat package of sentiments. But you do agree, don't you, Anderson, that the best thing to do is keep still?"

Elmer did, with reservations. "Unless, of course, something else comes up."

Now what did Elmer mean by that, Allegra asked herself on the way to her room with Olive—that the man was going to do it again, and maybe this time get his hands on her throat? Did Elmer mean another murder? Was he thinking of Olive?

Well, Foster McKane should be here tomorrow. He'd tell them what to do. Funny no one had mentioned his coming. Hadn't Olive...?

She turned abruptly to the other woman. "Did you tell the others you'd sent for Foster?"

Olive shook her head. "No need till we know when he's coming."

"Didn't you say tomorrow?" Allegra said.

"He said he'd *try* to make it tomorrow," Olive said.

Allegra groaned. If she could only be sure.

By the time they were both in bed and Olive fell asleep, Allegra's mood changed to one of irritation. Olive was secretive about the damnedest things: about sending for her lawyer, about expecting a cable (Had that cable come yet? If so, she hadn't told Allegra and maybe never would.), about extending their time in Carcassonne. It was information that would come out anyway in a day or two. And yet she'd talked her head off against her will, talked when she should have kept still, almost talked herself literally to death. And now here she was sleeping peacefully, even snoring a little in a ladylike way, while Allegra lay turning and turning.

She sat up and punched her pillow. That should get rid of some hostility, and what was more, she was going to have a sleeping pill. Let Olive take her chances tonight!

Chapter Nineteen

I t was Olive who saw the square of paper first and her exclamation brought Allegra, who was beginning to stir, fully awake.

"What's that piece of paper on the floor, Allegra?" she asked. "Looks like someone pushed it under the door. Funny they didn't knock."

Allegra sat up and her feet began groping for slippers. She recognized a hint when she heard one.

The square had been cut from a newspaper. She could see French words in lines, some of which had been cut through. She turned the clipping over and gasped.

Staggering to Olive's bed, she held it out. "Look! My God, look at that thing, Olive!"

It was a picture of the woman who had been killed, one of the after-death pictures. On the clipping a hand had been penciled in, gripping her throat. A penciled arrow pointed at it and, in large, childish block letters, had been printed: *VOUS!*

"What on earth?" It was Olive's strongest expression. "Doesn't that mean *you?*"

Olive placed the clipping on the bed.

"I wonder which one of us it's intended for? Not that it matters," Olive added. "It's bad either way. Thank heaven Foster's coming."

"I hope to God it'll be today," Allegra said fervently.

As if his name had triggered it, the telephone rang—those three or four quick jingles of European telephones.

This time Olive didn't hint that Allegra get it. Her hand darted out for the receiver before Allegra's did. "Yes, this is Madame Wallace. Cincinnati calling," she said. "Yes, yes, Foster, this is Olive. What? You can't? Oh, no! Tomorrow for sure. You've got your tickets? We need you desperately. Last night a Frenchman stopped Allegra and—no, he didn't do anything to her, but he was threatening... all right, I'll tell you tomorrow. And we got a picture—no, no, not something I bought. All right, I'll show you then. Be sure you get here."

She put the receiver back and sat staring at clenched hands. Finally they relaxed, and she turned to Allegra. "You heard. Foster's not coming till tomorrow."

Allegra nodded. She didn't have the energy for speech.

Olive picked up the receiver again and asked for Brian's room. "I won't need the car today, Brian," she told him when the connection had been made. "Tell Henry to get it ready for the Narbonne beach trip, and I'll have Allegra notify the others. What time do you want to leave?"

Then it was Allegra's turn to use the telephone. The last call was to order breakfast.

"They all said they'd be ready by eleven except Jen," she told Olive. "She doesn't want to go. Says she doesn't look so good in a bathing suit. The competition would be pretty strong with Cicely and Margot there. Sure you don't want to go, Olive? An afternoon on the beach might be relaxing."

"And let someone drown me in the Mediterranean? No thanks," Olive said.

Allegra and Olive both dressed and went downstairs to see the coach leave. Jen came down too, almost on their heels, and Allegra noticed that it wasn't only the glamorous Margot and super-glamorous Cicely who would show up Jen. Even Winifred, who was not a day younger than Jen, was as slim and appropriately curved as the girls. Poor Jen—but why was she saying poor Jen? Judging by her negligee and the voices Allegra had heard in the night, Jen was doing all right. And Winifred too, whom Allegra had thought of as prim... she remembered the pink negligee and the softly closing door. All this for Brian? What was going on? If she didn't have things on her mind that were more important—like life or death—she would give this intriguing situation more thought.

The coach drove away, jiggling over the cobblestones.

"Let's go look in the shops," Olive said. Her voice was almost girlish. "I've been so cooped up I've hardly seen Carcassonne."

There were two areas she avoided: the chateau, where she took one look at the stone steps and turned away, and the narrow street to the drawbridge, where a few nights ago she had almost been pushed under a tour bus.

When they returned to the hotel, Olive headed straight for the terrace. There, to Allegra's relief, she chose a table against the inside wall of the hotel.

The murder wasn't mentioned all morning. Neither was Allegra's experience of the night before. But Allegra kept a watchful eye on the people she met in the streets, on the people in the shops, and even those in passing cars. The face of the threatening man was not one of the faces she saw.

On the hotel terrace, she found herself looking closely at the faces of the waiters and in the hall at the bellboys.

Upstairs, Olive said to Jen, "Come on in and we can have some three-handed bridge."

Might as well be back in Cincinnati, Allegra thought, unless you looked out the window or heard the chambermaids and porters chattering French in the hall or remembered the body in the garbage can and that man's face last night.

Playing with Jen was apt to be slow while she dithered over the bidding. But she dithered effectively, Allegra conceded; Jen always made her bid and set any opponent she doubled.

Dithering now over what to lead, Jen sneezed and began to search for a tissue in her big handbag. The tissue was as elusive as her passport.

"Oh, for heaven's sake, Jen," Olive said, "use mine. It's in the top drawer of the dresser."

Standing at the chest of drawers with the top one open, Jen made a strange sound. Then she turned with a square of paper in her hand.

"My God, Olive, why do you keep this sort of thing around?" she said.

Olive and Allegra pushed back their chairs. Jen was holding out another picture like the one they had found on the floor this morning—a blurry, newspaper print of the dead woman with a hand drawn about her throat, the arrow, and the word *VOUS!* in large, childish print.

"How did it get there?" Olive's voice was a croak.

"Looks as if whoever shoved it under the door this morning has been in our room today," Allegra said, trying not to shiver visibly.

"There was one like this under your door this morning?" Jen asked.

"Yes," Allegra said.

"Did you report it to the concierge?" Jen asked.

"Not yet." Olive's voice was under control now. "It might be someone's idea of a joke."

"What's known as a macabre sense of humor," Allegra suggested feebly.

Jen brushed the joke idea aside. "Whoever put this in the drawer must have a key to your room," she said. "That means a chambermaid or a porter, and someone in charge at the hotel ought to know."

"They'd tell the police," Allegra said.

"Of course, they'd tell the police." For once, Jen was more assured than even Olive. "You know I said last night the police ought to be told about that man who threatened you, Allegra. If the local people are going around terrorizing tourists, the police ought to know. And the concierge ought to know about these pictures."

"Maybe—tomorrow," Olive said.

"Why tomorrow?" Jen demanded.

It was funny, thought Allegra, how Jen and Olive had reversed roles—Jen commanding, Olive temporizing. That is, it would be funny if the circumstances had been different.

She could see Olive making up her mind. When it was made up, Olive said, "Foster McKane's arriving tomorrow."

"Foster!" Jen exclaimed. "From Cincinnati?"

Olive nodded.

Jen looked like Jen again—vague and at the moment, bewildered. "Well, he should be a nice addition to the tour. Is his wife coming too?"

"It's not a social occasion, Jen," Olive scolded. "There've been some mighty peculiar things going on here, and I thought I'd feel more comfortable with Foster here. So, I sent for him. He's a lawyer and knows how to deal with the police, and he speaks French, you know."

"I know. Don't forget I work for him," Jen said. "I suppose in view of that threatening Frenchman last night, it was a good idea to send for him, and now with these threatening notes…" Jen paused. "Of course that murder makes us all nervous, even though it didn't have anything to do with us."

Now, what was Olive going to say? She played it cool. "We can't help being affected by it, as you say," Olive said. "But that man last night and these pictures—they're directly connected with us, and we may need legal advice."

For all Jen knew, it was Allegra's adventure of last night that made Olive call Foster. She had told Jen nothing to pass along to the others that would alert anyone, nothing about mistaken identity.

The three women sat down at the table again, but all inclination for bridge had vanished. All any of them could see was that square newspaper clipping.

Olive's arm went out and she swept up the cards. "Why don't you two go for a walk, or take a taxi over to the new town, or do something that will take you away for an hour or so. Before Foster comes, I want to get my thoughts organized."

"Nothing personal, then?" Jen said.

My God, thought Allegra, Jen could be coy even with Olive.

"I won't have any time to myself after the others get back," Olive said. "Don't you want to mail that letter on the writing table, Allegra?"

"What letter?" Allegra asked. "Oh, that. I thought it was something of yours. I'd be glad to mail it."

"It's not mine," Olive said.

The three women were on their feet again. Allegra got to the writing table first. The envelope was unaddressed and unsealed. Inside was another picture of the woman who had been killed, with the penciled hand, the arrow, the *VOUS!*—exactly like the other two.

"It never occurred to me to open it," Olive mumbled. "I wonder how long it's been there."

"You saw it when we came in?" Allegra asked.

"I did," Jen said. "I remember thinking, 'Too bad Allegra didn't get her letter mailed while we were out.'"

"I saw it too," Olive said, "as soon as we came in."

"I didn't notice it," Allegra said, "and I'm sure it wasn't there when we went down to see the bus off. I left my bag on that table last night, and when I picked it up this morning there wasn't anything else there. You can't help noticing something white like that. It's one of the hotel envelopes."

"Come to think of it, I didn't see it before we went downstairs either," Olive said. "When we came in, I automatically thought it was yours because it wasn't mine."

"It has to be someone working here who left it," Jen insisted, "someone with a key."

"I don't think I want to go out now, Olive," Allegra said, "and leave you here by yourself with these ghastly pictures showing up."

"Nonsense," Olive returned. "Don't forget the first one came under the door."

"But now we know he has a key—" Jen stopped. "We couldn't stand it if anything happened to you, Olive dear."

"Nonsense," Olive said again, and this time Allegra almost said it too; Jen was really sickening. "I still have to organize my thoughts before Foster arrives. I'll wedge a chair under the doorknob."

They left it that way, going with reluctance. Allegra looked at her watch on the way out and they allowed Olive only the hour she asked for. Both were relieved when her voice answered Jen's knock.

As they heard the chair being taken away from the doorknob, Jen said, "I think I'll go to my room for a while, now I know Olive's all right. But, for God's sake, take care."

For the first time since the morning, Olive and Allegra were alone.

"Look, Olive—" Allegra could hardly wait until the door was closed "—I didn't want to say this in front of Jen, but it didn't have to be someone with a key who put those pictures in our room. A key would have to be involved, of course, but you know how the chambermaids sometimes open up two or three rooms at once? I suppose they think it's more efficient to do the same type of thing in two or three rooms without having to change tools. Well, why couldn't whoever had those pictures whip into this room, drop the pictures, and whip out again while the maid was next door."

"He'd be taking quite a chance," Olive said.

"Sure he'd be taking a chance," Allegra echoed. "But if it was the man who stopped me last night, he doesn't mind taking chances. And he probably has some kind of in with the chambermaids if he had any connection with the girl who was killed. Maybe he's mixed up in the nylon racket too."

"Hm-m," Olive said thoughtfully. "If it was someone who slipped in while the door was open, it wouldn't have to be that Frenchman. It could be anyone in the hotel. I noticed that both Winifred and Brian went back inside before they left for Narbonne—Winifred first, and she had hardly come back to the car when Brian went in. I thought they were paying a last visit to the bathroom."

"But why would they want to plant those pictures in our room, Olive?" Allegra said. "What possible advantage could they get out of it?"

"You were the one who suggested someone might have mistaken that French girl for me," Olive said. "If that's the case, why couldn't that someone be trying to throw suspicion somewhere else—to suggest it being a French crime that has nothing to do with any of us?"

"You may have something there, Olive!" Allegra said. "The old lady came to do our room when we went downstairs, and both Jen and Cicely got to the bus later than we did. Either one of them could have left the pictures, or Winifred or Brian later. I hadn't thought of that."

"I'll certainly be glad when Foster gets here," Olive said. "By the way, he said he sent that cable I was expecting before he knew he was coming himself. It was delayed somehow, but I got it a while ago while you were out with Jen. So far, we've been indulging in speculation, but the cable gave me some news you'll be interested in. I asked Foster to run down all the information he could get on Cicely."

"Information on Cicely?" Allegra sounded surprised.

"I didn't know anything about her when she and Elmer were married, and I can't say either one of them has been particularly communicative on this trip," Olive said. "If I'm going to leave a lot of money to Elmer, I want to know more about his wife. The first word I got soon after we reached Carcassonne was that there was no such person at the address she had given when they applied for a marriage license."

"I suppose there could be a lot of reasons—" Allegra began.

"There certainly could," Olive said tartly, "and one of them was the reason I got today. She'd done time, if you call it that, in a girls' reformatory for shoplifting."

How could Olive look so triumphant? The same news made Allegra sick. Poor Cicely, poor Elmer, who plodded patiently into every shop with his beautiful young wife. No wonder. He didn't dare let her go in by herself.

Well, at least Cicely couldn't be suspected of stabbing that French girl—the girl wearing Olive's suit. Why not? asked a cold judicial voice in the back of Allegra's head. Elmer had gone out. There was no one to say Cicely hadn't dressed and gone out too. Gone out long enough to stab the woman she thought was Olive, who would leave her husband a lot of money, and whip back into the hotel again and her frothy green negligee. Give a dog a bad name...

Allegra, Olive, and Cicely were the only ones who hadn't been out that morning. But Cicely could have, and, for God's sake, so could Olive! Her alibi was Allegra, and Allegra had been sound asleep.

So Olive stabbed the woman who wore her suit—thinking it was Olive, no doubt? How silly can you get? But was that any sillier than thinking kitten like, indolent Cicely would get out of bed, dress, kill, undress, and go to bed again? Yes, a lot sillier. Cicely might be lazy, but money was important to her.

Dinner was late that night. The bus came back from Narbonne late, full of hungry, sunburned people who had evidently had their before-dinner drinks on the way home— they were all so noisy and cheerful. That made it easier for Allegra to face Cicely and Elmer, whom she was now seeing in a new light—although on the surface, at least, it was no different from the old light.

Jen was obviously feeling left out, but soon became the center of attention. "Guess who's coming tomorrow!" she said, coyly looking at Brian.

He couldn't.

"Foster McKane!"

"Who's he? Cicely asked.

"Isn't he your lawyer, Olive?" Margot asked.

The others hadn't needed to ask. They all sat still, looking at Olive.

"Why?" Winifred asked sharply.

Neither Brian nor Elmer spoke. The eyes of all five remained fixed on Olive.

Jen made another bid for attention. "After what happened to Allegra and Cicely last night, and then after what Olive and Allegra found today—did you people know about the pictures?"

"What pictures?" That was Winifred's sharp voice again.

"A newspaper picture of the woman who was murdered, with a hand drawn around her throat and—" Jen interrupted. "Don't you have one with you, Olive?"

"Not here," she said. "If you want to come to my room after dinner, I'll show you."

Once upstairs, Olive took them out of the handbag she had had with her at dinner. All three pictures were together, protected by a fold of hotel letter paper. She started one going to her right and one to her left around the circle.

Holding a picture in his hand, Brian looked up. "Why didn't you want to show us these at the table, Olive?"

"The waiters are always hovering," she said. "They'd see, and word would get around."

"Maybe word ought to get around," Elmer said slowly, "like to the police. I don't like this—intimidation."

"Who does?" Olive said, her face grim. "But since Foster McKane will be here tomorrow and he's a lawyer, I thought I'd wait for legal advice. I don't want to get involved with the police in a foreign country without it."

"How wonderful that you can afford to bring an American lawyer clear over here, Olive," Jen said admiringly, as if the ability to pay were something to be credited solely to Olive's brilliance. "Think of all the little people who come from other countries and perhaps inadvertently step on French toes—think of what they might have to go through."

"That's what I *don't* want to go through," Olive said briskly. "Brian, we'll drive to Toulouse tomorrow morning, have lunch, and pick up Foster at the airfield. Tell Henry so he can have the car ready."

There were two tables of bridge that night, the first time there had been two on the tour. Nobody wanted to go out, not even Margot, though two or three times Henri hovered in the doorway to give her a chance to change her mind. Probably, Allegra told herself as she lost a trick she could have taken, they were all thinking of that hand on the pictured throat, and no one wanted it to be laid on a real one, especially his or her own.

It was eleven-thirty before the bridge players went upstairs. A wild night for early-to-bed Olive, Allegra mused.

But there was more in store for them both, as she discovered when she sat down at the writing table. Tonight, she didn't dare to take a sleeping pill, so Bob Jr. would get another letter.

She pulled open the drawer to find a sheet of paper and found the fourth clipping.

"Olive," she said. Her voice was strained.

Olive, whose nightgown was halfway over her head, emerged walking. "What is it? What's the matter, Allegra? Not another one of those pictures!"

They both stood looking into the drawer. As Olive started to reach, Allegra caught her hand. "Wait! We didn't think about fingerprints. The other clippings have been handled by everybody. I'll get the tweezers and when I lift the clipping, you pull out a sheet of paper and fold it, as you did for the others. Put it in your handbag for Foster without touching the clipping."

It was only after this maneuver had been accomplished that they thought about ways and means of the clipping's arrival.

"I suppose the chambermaid or porter or whoever got busy with his key again while we were playing bridge or having dinner," Olive said.

"Or if the point you made is right, about one of our own group throwing suspicion on someone local, it would have been easy tonight," Allegra said. "Everyone was in here, and it would have been easy to slip a picture into the drawer while everyone else was absorbed in looking at the first three."

"Or it could even have been planted with the other two," Olive said. "I haven't looked in this drawer since yesterday. Have you?"

Allegra shook her head.

Olive set down her handbag with a thump.

"I don't know about you, but I'm going to bed," she said. "If this had been the first picture we'd found, I probably wouldn't get a wink of sleep. As it is, they're an old story."

"But I'll bet you're still glad Foster's coming tomorrow," Allegra said.

"I can't tell you what a relief it is," Olive said.

Nevertheless, Olive, as usual, went right to sleep.

Allegra made another entry in her tour journal, wrote to her son, got ready for bed, and was propped up reading when she heard a soft knock on the door.

It was one o'clock. She looked at Olive, who was still asleep. Well, Allegra told herself, she jolly well wouldn't open the door until she found out who it was.

It was Winifred's voice in the hall, speaking softly. "Let me in, Allegra. Hurry!"

When Allegra opened the door, Winifred whipped through without fully closing it behind her. Allegra reached toward it, and Winifred hissed—hissed was the only word—"No, leave it open a little and if you see Brian, let me know."

"What's the matter?" Allegra asked. "Is Brian up to something? Look out, you'll wake Olive."

"I've got to," Winifred said. "I can't stand this any longer. And I won't."

Tonight, for the first time in Allegra's existence, Winifred's face looked crumpled. She walked quickly to Olive's bed and shook her bare shoulder where it came, with the strap of her nightgown, above the blanket.

Olive gave a jerk, then sat up so suddenly Winifred jumped back. "Wha—What's the matter? Who's been killed?"

"No one's been killed," Winifred said. "But I have to tell you something. Let you see for yourself. Look, Olive—"

"What on earth's the matter?" Olive was awake now. "What in the world did you wake me up for in the middle of the night?"

"Sh-h-h," Winifred cautioned. "He'll hear you. Or she will."

"What are you talking about?" Olive said.

"Sh-h-h," Winifred said again. "You've got to know. I can't keep it bottled up any longer."

"Know what?" Olive demanded irritably.

"Every night, about this time, Brian goes to her room in his bathrobe and—" Winifred began.

"Whose room?" Olive interrupted.

"Jen's. And he stays—" Winifred said.

"Winifred!" Olive exploded. "You don't know what you're saying!"

"I know only too well," Winifred returned fiercely, "In addition to it being immoral conduct—"

"Oh, come now," Allegra interrupted. "Jen's forty-three years old and Brian must be thirty-five. And neither one's married. Who're they harming?"

Winifred went right on as if there had been no interruption. "—it's adulterous immoral conduct."

"Adulterous?" Olive's voice squeaked.

"You mean one of them's married?" Allegra gasped. "Brian?"

Winifred nodded.

"How do you know?" Allegra said.

"I'm Brian's wife," Winifred whispered.

When she saw Olive sitting with her mouth open, Allegra realized that hers was too. Her eyes went involuntarily to Winifred's left hand. There was the gold wedding band, that may or may not have been her mother's, on Winifred's wedding-ring finger.

"Are you out of your mind?" Olive demanded. Vigor had returned to her voice.

"I was when I married him," Winifred said bitterly. "You know how attractive he is and how persuasive he can be. Sh-h-h, here he comes!" She had returned to her post by the slightly open door and was beckoning wildly. "Turn out the light!"

Allegra wasn't having any part of this. She sat down on the edge of her bed.

It was Olive who turned out the light and tiptoed over to the door. Before it was closed, Allegra heard a light knock and the click of another door latch.

"Did you see that negligee she had on?" Winifred demanded. "Receiving my husband in that... my husband..."

"But, Winifred, when—?" Olive asked weakly.

"Three months ago, in St. Louis," Winifred said.

"But—you were still Miss Jenkins in Cincinnati," Olive said. "Brian was still in my house. Why didn't you tell me?" Olive looked outraged.

"You know the current Board doesn't want its librarians married, not even its assistant librarians," Winifred explained. "You got me the job. With your strong conscience, you'd feel you had to tell the Board if we told you. And we need both salaries. Brian can't support himself and a nonworking wife in the sort of place where you'd like to have the first families of Cincinnati meet your only first cousin. And then, with this trip coming up, Brian said—"

Olive bored in. "Brian said what?"

"He said if we told you, then it was like hinting to turn the tour into a wedding trip for us," Winifred said. "He thought it would be a lot more tactful if he seemed to be a single man instead of a bridegroom. He thought you'd feel more comfortable about calling on him for various chores, and we should wait till we got home before we told you."

"But how would telling her this improve anything?" Allegra asked. "Your situation would still be the same. If you really need two salaries to live on, you'll still need them when we get back from Europe."

Olive's face darkened as Winifred stumbled through her excuses. By the time Allegra asked her question, it was almost purple. "It's obvious Brian was counting on the situation changing," Olive said, her voice as congested as her face. "If he was lucky, I'd die on this trip, and he'd be married to a rich wife."

"Olive! What a dreadful thing to say!" Winifred cried.

"Not as dreadful as to act on the idea," Olive said harshly.

"What do you mean?" Winifred's voice sharpened.

"Brian might have been trying to make sure," Olive said. "Maybe he was the one who arranged those accidents."

"He caught you on the stairs in Nîmes, Olive!" Winifred objected. "How can you say that? Why, Brian—Brian worships you. He's always been so grateful for what you've done."

"Come to think of it," Olive looked at Allegra, "it was Brian who put the whole idea of this trip into my head. I like to think of it as entirely my idea... but it was really Brian's. He must have been planning it even then. Planning those accidents..." She turned furiously back to Winifred. "I can't understand how you'd do such a thing anyway, Winifred Jenkins—or should I say Winifred Gifford? Sneaking off to get married behind my back—my own cousin and the young man I took out of a bare-existence job and gave a position of prestige with a wonderful future—the young man I took into my own home—" Olive's words were flowing so fast she began to stutter.

"Don't forget I *am* your own cousin, Olive, your own first cousin," Winifred said. "I'm your nearest relative and Brian loves you like a son. Neither of us would do anything to hurt you for the world. Brian thought it was best for you not to—"

Olive's tongue had recovered its equilibrium. "Well, you can tell Brian—" She stopped suddenly.

"We thought what we were doing was best for you," Winifred said. "We didn't want to spoil your lovely generous gesture of giving us all a trip to Europe—a luxury trip, by making it into a wedding trip for two out of the group—stealing your thunder..."

Stealing Olive's thunder... trust Brian to hit the nail on the head. Allegra shook hers.

"Think it over, Olive," Winifred continued. "Allegra, help her see it from our point of view. You've always been fair-minded. I won't say anything more now; it seems to upset her."

That might be the understatement of the year, but it showed more powers of observation than Allegra knew Winifred had.

She slid out of the room even more quietly than she'd come in.

"Sneaking off to get married behind my back," Olive muttered. "Those ungrateful—Brian was after the money I'd leave Winifred in my will. Her own tongue convicted them... saying they had to have two salaries and couldn't

149

tell me because I'd tell the Board… and then saying they were going to tell me when we get home… you noticed it yourself when you asked her how going home would change the situation. They were counting on my not going home. One of those accidents would see to that. It's their only way out. And the will would leave Winifred a rich woman married to Brian… well, I'll see about that. Hand me my yellow tablet, will you, Allegra."

Olive was still muttering when the tablet was put into her hand.

"And that Jen—" Her diamonds flashed as she fished in her handbag for a pen "—getting involved with a married man…"

"I doubt if she knew he was married," Allegra said gently, "to give her credit."

"Credit!" Olive snorted.

For once, Allegra went to sleep first. She left Olive sitting at the writing table, her right arm sliding furiously back and forth across the paper.

Chapter Twenty

The bus was halfway to Toulouse before Jen became sufficiently perturbed to get up from her seat behind Olive and move across the aisle to sit down by Allegra.

"What's the matter with Olive?" Jen asked. "She doesn't pay the slightest attention to anything I say. She only grunts, if she takes even that much notice. Have I upset her in some way?"

"I'm afraid you have," Allegra said dryly. "She found out about last night."

Jen still looked mystified.

"You and Brian," Allegra amplified.

Jen groaned. She knew Olive as well as Allegra did.

"I guess I ought to tell you something else," Allegra hesitated. "Did you know that Brian is married?"

"He's *what?*" Jen's head jerked up and her glasses slid down her nose.

"He and Winifred—in St. Louis—three months ago," Allegra said.

They sat in stony silence until Jen began to speak again as if she were talking in her sleep. "And to think I got him to come in that first night by threatening to tell Olive I'd seen him come out of Winifred's room."

So, it was Jen's door Allegra had heard the night she too had seen Brian come out of Winifred's room.

"I'd never tell anyone but you, Allegra, that I had to blackmail a man into—coming to my room," Jen said.

Poor Jen. Allegra remembered the afternoon she'd almost bumped into her coming out of Brian's room and how triumphant she'd looked. Jen, the successful blackmailer.

151

"I won't tell anyone," Allegra said gently.

"At least I never had to apply any pressure after the first night," Jen said with a blush.

Allegra patted the tense hand in the lap next to hers.

Eventually Jen spoke again. "And to think he was paying his wife what you might call a marital visit... I wonder why they kept quiet."

"Winifred's job, for one thing," Allegra said.

Jen nodded. "And Olive's will. It's not a marriage she'd like, and she might be mad enough to cut Winifred out... and Brian too, if he was ever in."

Jen was silent again. After a while, still in silence, she moved back to the seat across the aisle and turned her face toward the window.

Allegra turned hers toward the window on her side. The hedge-smooth vineyard they were passing was nothing but a blur of green.

Inside the coach, the same people filled the same seats they had sat in ever since the Andersons had been picked up in Marseilles, but the tension in the coach seemed different. The earlier chatter and laughter may have been forced, but at least it was there. There was no laughter now. Behind her Allegra could hear Cicely talking to Elmer, but hers was the only audible voice on the bus. In front of Allegra, Margot was dividing her attention between the window and Henri's back. In the director's seat next to Henri, Brian wasn't bringing anyone's attention to points of interest today. He sat with bent head, in glum silence. Winifred must have told him about last night. Behind him, in the first passenger seat, Olive was still wrapped in silent outrage. Behind her, Jen's face remained window-ward, shoulders bunched tightly, and behind her, a straight-lipped Winifred kept clenching her hands, clenching and unclenching...

My God, Allegra thought, what a trip this turned out to be!

Almost in her ear, making Allegra jump, Cicely said brightly, "Tomorrow's our last full day in Carcassonne, isn't it?"

"Yes," Allegra said. The voices sounded loud in the silent coach.

"Are you glad or sorry?" Cicely was still being brightly chatty.

"I'm afraid I'm glad," Allegra admitted.

No one else spoke. No one turned to look. Even Cicely fell silent.

152

The bus rolled on through bright sunshine that should have been rain, Allegra thought, better yet thunder and lightning.

In Toulouse, lunch was a frigid affair, with Cicely and Elmer, Margot, and Allegra doing all the talking. The others barely answered when spoken to.

When Foster McKane got off his plane, Allegra thought she hadn't been so glad to see anyone since Bob was alive.

Driving back, Foster sat in the seat with Olive, and the murmur of their bass and alto was the only sound in the coach. Even Cicely and Elmer were silent. They were all, Allegra thought, trying to hear what was being said. She strained to hear also, hoping against anxious hope that Olive would remember all the flapping ears about her and that Foster wouldn't ask anything that should be answered only in private. The words she could hear were innocent enough.

Occasionally the others broke in with a "Have-you-told-him-about" question, and once or twice Margot tried from across the aisle to point out some of the passing countryside.

When they came in sight of Carcassonne, the window claimed Foster's whole attention. Walls and turrets rose above the vineyards as if, for a few seconds, the ground had cracked open, and the Middle Ages overflowed.

"Well, there are other things to France besides Paris!" Foster exclaimed. "Do they fit you with a suit of armor at the drawbridge?"

For what was left of the afternoon, Olive was in conference with her lawyer while Allegra wandered about the Cité to leave their hotel room free. She met most of her fellow tour members also wandering, looking both aimless and nervous.

Cicely stopped her near the traffic light and expressed what Allegra felt was foremost in the thoughts of them all. "I suppose she's changing her will again."

Elmer, at his wife's side, said quickly, "Not necessarily, honey. She and McKane have plenty to talk over, with this man who threatened you and Allegra and all these threatening pictures they've been finding. I've been wondering whether the police will let us leave, if McKane decides they have to be told. It seems as if there must be some connection with the murder. It's

153

too much to think such events aren't related. Too bad you girls aren't more proficient in French so you could tell what that fellow was saying."

"I still think they're having a will-changing session," Cicely said firmly. "Olive's furious at Brian and Winifred for getting married without telling her, or for simply getting married, in my opinion. And now, of course, she's mad at Jen too. I told you about last night, Elmer."

"Gossip, gossip, gossip," Elmer said. "That's women for you. Sorry about that, Allegra."

"It's no news to Allegra," Cicely said. She was there. I must say I feel for them—those who are getting cut out—but I hope that what she takes away from them she gives to us."

"Cicely, for God's sake!" Elmer's big hand clamped down on her arm and he began to pull her away.

"Well, somebody has to benefit," she responded. Over her shoulder, Cicely winked at Allegra.

The fact that Olive had done a lot of writing last night was something only she and Allegra knew. Whether all that writing meant the will had already been changed was something only Olive knew, and maybe, by now, Foster McKane.

At six-thirty, Allegra decided she had given Olive and Foster enough time to get private business over with. He might want to ask Allegra some questions too, and in any event, it was time to begin cleaning up for dinner. When the dining room opened, the Wallace party was usually waiting at the door.

Tonight, it was not, even though Allegra was late.

When she went upstairs after hours of tramping the cobblestones, Foster had already left.

He was tired, Olive told her. "You know how you are when you're on a plane all night and then wait at the airport for another, and the difference in time and all."

Foster had gone to stretch out for a while before dinner. He wanted to think over what Olive had told him before deciding what they should do. Yes, she had told him about the accidents, whether they had any connection with the murder or not, and she had told him about the murdered woman wearing her suit and the others not knowing she had given it away. Yes, she showed him the pictures; she had done that on the bus.

Allegra wanted to see him alone herself before he made up his mind, but surely that could be arranged after dinner. Meanwhile, she wanted a quick tub and a change of clothes.

When she came out of the bathroom, Olive was gone too. Funny what a difference Foster McKane's arrival had made. Yesterday her absence would have worried Allegra. Today it meant only that Olive hadn't waited for Allegra to go down to dinner.

Even though Olive wasn't there when Allegra reached the dining room, she wasn't worried. The urgency of her feeling of responsibility had lessened to such an extent that Olive's absence was no more alarming than any of the others', and they were all absent. She sat down in the long hall to wait.

Olive, too, must feel less concern now that Foster was here. When she came in this afternoon, Allegra had not had to use her key for the first time in days.

But it was odd that no one had arrived. It was almost quarter of nine. As she looked at her watch, Cicely and Elmer came in from the direction of the cocktail lounge, and Margot and Henri from the square. Behind them Jen came in, breathless and windblown.

Elmer was full of news. "What do you know, the police have arrested the boyfriend of that French girl who was killed! Seems he's been stopping women tourists and raving about how Marie would still be alive if it wasn't for them and trying to get money out of them because he says he can't work, and Marie was suffocating him and—"

"What do you want to bet that's the man who stopped us, Allegra?" Cicely interrupted. "That must have been what he was saying when—"

"Announcing to the fellow we were talking to in the bar," broke in Elmer, "he is off his rocker because he swears a tourist killed her and the police haven't been able to sort out whether he means that literally or whether he's referring to the temptation provided by the tourists in the shape of nylons and that kind of thing."

Suddenly, Brian and Winifred hurried in the outside door.

"Where's Olive?" Brian looked at his watch. "And McKane? I thought we were late."

"Still in conference?" Winifred suggested. She put a determined smile on her face.

"Don't they stop for dinner?" Margot asked. "We're awfully late."

"They weren't in our room when I came down," Allegra said. She still wasn't worried.

"Then they're probably in McKane's," Elmer said. "I'll go up and tell them it's time for dinner."

He came back quickly, frowning. "McKane was there but he'd gone to sleep. Said he hasn't seen Olive since he left her room this afternoon. You're sure she's not there, Allegra?"

"She wasn't fifteen minutes ago," Allegra said. "I'll run up and see if she's back."

She didn't wait for the elevator. Running up the stairs, her heart bumping, she remembered the other time she had half run and half stumbled with a bumping heart up these stairs—the morning she had seen the group at the garbage can and the body in Olive's suit. Oh, forget it, she told herself fiercely. There's no murder now. Olive's all right.

At her door, the key wouldn't fit this time either. She pounded on it, shouting, "Olive!" When the key finally did go in, Olive wasn't there.

As she came out, Foster McKane closed the door of his room.

"Don't wait for the elevator," she told him. "The stairs—we can't find Olive."

"Don't get excited, Allegra," Foster said. "She probably stepped outside. It's a beautiful evening. We'll find her."

If it hadn't been for him—if Foster's presence hadn't made Allegra relax her guard—it had probably had the same effect on Olive.

Downstairs in the long hall, the others were still waiting, standing in a tight little knot. Allegra shook her head.

Foster took charge. "Why don't each of you look in your rooms in case she might have wanted to see you privately for some reason and be waiting for you there. Then if you don't find her, we'll meet down here and plan a systematic search."

"Oh, the wall!" Allegra cried. The wall she had tried so hard to keep Olive away from.

She shot down the side hall and out the door to the terrace, between the tables, to the edge. She sucked in a deep breath and looked over.

Her breath came out again. There was no one crumpled at the foot of the wall.

There was no one in the hall but Foster McKane. As she joined him, the others began to trickle back, each one with a headshake.

"Olive must have gone out for a breath of air. Taken a little walk—" Foster began.

"The chateau!" Jen cried. "Those deep shadows—"

"It's not dark enough yet," Winifred objected.

"If the lights are turned on, there'll be shadows." Allegra remembered the black shade on each side of the gate and shivered.

"I'll look." Brian began to run. Out the door, past the windows…

Henri followed, also at a run.

"Perhaps she's in the cathedral," Margot said, and began to run across the square in the other direction.

Elmer's friend, the camera bug, came in the door with his neck draped, as usual, with cameras. He twisted to look at Margot. "What's going on, Anderson? Everybody running around like crazy…"

"We can't find Olive, our hostess… you know, Mrs. Wallace."

"Is that anything to get so excited about?" the camera bug said. "Isn't she the lady with the bad ankle? I saw her about half an hour ago getting into your bus. The sun had gone down, and I was experimenting…"

He found he was talking to himself. Everyone else—both Andersons, Allegra and Foster, Jen and Winifred, were all streaming across the square.

The bus was parked by the wall, behind several other cars which cut off the view of the door. Another coach beside it, a larger tour bus, darkened the windows. But even when they got past the first bus, there was no one to be seen through the windows of theirs.

"She's not there," Elmer said.

"Try the door!" Allegra cried. "She may be—"

Foster reached for the handle. "It's locked. She can't be there."

"But he said he saw her getting in," Allegra argued. "Only half an hour ago—that's the last time anyone saw her. We've got to look. Who has a key?"

"Olive did, you know," Winifred said. "Otherwise, I guess it's Henri and Brian."

The camera bug caught up with them. "I told Anderson about my hobby of snapping women getting into cars—buses and private automobiles," he said. "Sometimes I get some pretty entertaining pictures to show later. I've been experimenting with light, and it was twilight enough when she was getting in to be a challenge—sort of kill two birds with one stone. She doesn't seem to be there now."

"When did you say you saw her get in?" Winifred asked.

He looked at his watch. "It was exactly…" He went on muttering to himself, then looked up triumphantly. "Exactly thirty-six and one-half minutes ago. But there was someone else with her. She wasn't by herself."

"Who?" Allegra found she was holding her breath.

"That lady." He nodded at Jen.

"Why didn't you tell us, Jen?" Allegra demanded.

"I—I thought she came out," Jen stammered. "She was right behind me."

"You didn't wait for her?" Allegra asked.

"No. She told me to go on," Jen said. "She thought of something she wanted to get while she was here, and she's been so—so unfriendly today I didn't want to hang around. I bought some handkerchiefs in Toulouse and left the package in the bus and then I wished I'd brought them in, so when Olive came along—I knew she had a key—so I asked her if she'd let me in."

"Why didn't you tell us?" Allegra cried again.

"It seemed so long ago," Jen said. "And Olive was on her way out. She was going to pick up a package and lock the door."

"Did you see her go into the hotel?" Allegra said.

"No, but—the bus door's locked," Jen said. "She must have gone in when I stopped to look at the cathedral. It was beautiful in the evening light, and I must have stood there quite a while looking at it—"

"Here's Brian!" Winifred cried.

"Will you unlock the bus, Gifford?" Foster asked.

Henri was behind Brian and Margot had come out of the cathedral, shaking her head, so the entire Wallace tour was together when they found Olive. She was lying on her face on the floor of the bus with a knife like the one that had killed the French woman sticking out of her back.

All of them crowded into the bus but Margot and Henri, who stood on the cobblestones with a protective arm around her. The one outsider, the camera bug, stood beside them.

In the bus, Allegra asked hoarsely, "A—doctor?"

Foster had been kneeling trying to find Olive's pulse. He stood up. "There's no use. We'll have to call the police. But first—" His voice rose, stopping the stir in the group near the door "—there are some things I need to get straight while I can talk to all of you. This'll be the last time."

"The last time?" Winifred echoed. "What do you mean?"

"One of you is going to be arrested," Foster explained.

There was a seething silence in the bus. Then Cicely repeated weakly, "A—arrested? One of us?"

"Who do you think planned an accident to kill Olive?" Foster asked. "Some mysterious Frenchman who followed you all the way from Marseilles to Avignon to Nîmes to Carcassonne? That fellow collaring Allegra the other night was a real break for one of you. Jen, you were the last to admit seeing Olive in the bus. Assuming she was alive when you left—"

"My God, Foster, what are you saying—that I'd kill my oldest friend?" Jen asked. "Why, I've known Olive ever since I was born—"

"I know, Jen. So have I." Foster's voice was more gentle. "After you got out of the bus, was it still unlocked?"

"The door was standing open," Jen said. "I walked over to the edge of the parked cars, or maybe I wasn't all the way past the cars, but I got to a place where the cathedral showed up clearly and I stood there gawking at it, not paying attention to anything else. You know how I am."

"You didn't hear footsteps or voices?" Foster asked.

"No. I didn't hear anything," Jen said.

"Not even the slam of a car door?" Foster asked.

Jen shook her head.

Foster looked at the people crowded into the front of the bus. "Allegra said none of you were on hand when she came down between eight-thirty and quarter of nine. Anderson, where were you before you came in for dinner?"

"Cicely and I were waiting for dinner in the cocktail lounge—together," Elmer finished firmly.

"Together all the time?" Foster asked.

"Together all the time," Elmer confirmed.

Foster turned to the woman behind Elmer. "Where were you, Winifred?"

"Out walking. I went up the hill behind the post office and downtown," she said.

"Alone?"

"Until I ran into Brian on the way back," Winifred said.

"Did you see anyone else you knew?" Foster asked.

As Winifred said, "No, so I can't prove it," Allegra found herself thinking he was asking the very things she had asked after the murder of the French girl, but Foster didn't have to veil his questions, and those he was asking questions of knew what hung on the answers.

"Brian?"

"Yes, McKane, I met Winifred, as she said. Before that I was walking around too. I did stop for cigarettes, but I've no idea whether the man who sold them to me will remember."

Foster leaned toward the door and called, "Margot."

The girl raised her dark head from Henri's shoulder and came closer, keeping a tight hold on his hand.

"How and where did you wait out the time before dinner?" Foster asked.

Her face showed she had been crying, but her voice was steady. "I was with Henri. We were wandering around the side streets."

Foster McKane sighed. "The French police will check your alibis, I suppose, but I'll be able to tell them who to arrest."

"You will?" Allegra asked faintly.

"There are only three of you who could have—done this." For a moment he looked down and hesitated. "And only one of you... it took a highly organized mind to turn the situation at the Pont d'Avignon and the duel in the Nîmes Colosseum and the traffic on the narrow streets of Carcassonne into possible fatal accidents. An organized mind to take advantage of catching Olive alone behind the hotel—it looked like Olive in a suit everyone knew was hers. A mind that no matter how organized was oddly insensitive in one way, never *en rapport* with others', never quite attuned to them, or it would have asked itself, before plunging the knife into that French girl, why Olive would be looking into one of the hotel garbage cans—"

"Hey, Anderson!" interrupted the camera bug who kept coming closer and was now on the bottom step craning into the bus. "Tell him, I took some pictures that morning that will interest him. At the back corner of the hotel. I was going to give them to the police till I saw there weren't any local people in them. It didn't occur to me then..." He broke off and metaphorically changed his lens. "I was experimenting with early morning light..."

No one was listening, and his voice trailed away.

Everyone's eyes were fixed on Foster McKane, who went right on as if there had been no interruption. "The organized mind even took advantage of that wild Frenchman's harangue to send those clippings with one French word printed on them to throw suspicion away from any of you. Don't think it wasn't well planned. And even tonight..."

Allegra heard herself swallow.

"Tonight, there were only three of you who had a chance to kill Olive—Brian, Winifred, and Jen—the only ones who were outdoors alone. But only one of them had the lack of information and the type of mind—" He paused, and all eyes turned toward Winifred.

"Well, at least you're in the clear, Jen," Cicely said. "No one could accuse you of having an organized mind."

"On the contrary, Mrs. Anderson," Foster contradicted. "Anyone who's ever worked with Jen knows the fine quality of her mind. Losing her passport—all that vague befuddlement—it's nothing but protective coloring. She needs—"

Jen interrupted. "What do you mean when you said one of us lacked information?"

"Winifred knew last night that Olive knew about the whole situation and was furiously angry with all three of you," Foster said. "Winifred would know that all three names were coming out of the will—and fast. And what Winifred knew Brian knew, probably, before breakfast this morning. But you didn't find out, Jen, till you were in the bus on the way to Toulouse that Olive knew about your last night's activities and Winifred and Brian's marriage."

Jen was staring at him, frozen.

"At the time of the accidents and the French woman's murder, you were well provided for in Olive's will. But now—it's too late, Jen," Foster said.

"You don't mean a new will's already been written?" Jen's voice sounded strangled.

Foster nodded without speaking.

"I thought, since you were coming today, she'd wait to have it done right, by you. I knew you'd have to get a secretary with a typewriter..." Jen's voice died away and then came so softly that Allegra could hardly hear it. "I had to do it tonight."

"You were right about her wanting me to draw a new will, Jen," Foster said. "But to be covered in the interim she wrote out what she wanted last night. It'll stand in any court of law, Jen."

Out of that frozen face Jen said hoarsely, "Nothing ever goes right for me."

Foster sighed. "Now we must call the police."

The End

P.S. If you enjoyed the book, please leave post a review on the site where you purchased it. You are welcome to visit my website at www.ElizabethReedAden.com to learn more about personalized medicine and my other books.

A Note from the Author

Eunice Mays Boyd was my, Elizabeth Reed Aden's, godmother.

When Eunice, or "Nana", died on February 4, 1971, she left me many things. Some jewelry, a framed *Pennsylvania Gazette* from 1758, and unpublished manuscripts. When the estate was settled and the articles in the will were distributed, I was in graduate school on the East Coast. My mother relieved me of the burdens of dealing with Nana's bequests and stored my inheritance safely at her house for decades.

At the time of Nana's death, she was working on a novel set primarily in Carcassonne, in the south of France. I read a draft of that novel in 1970, and she left me her working draft in a clipboard. I kept those hundreds of yellowed pages with me in a safe place for the next 40 years. In 2014, my husband Mel and I traveled to Europe, and I insisted we visit Carcassonne. After Mel returned to the States, I reread a scanned copy of her book set in the restored medieval walled city. I stayed at one of the hotels Nana mentioned and visited some of the places Nana described. I communed with her that day in April over croissants and café au lait.

When my mother died in 2016, I discovered three more of Eunice's unpublished novels in a cardboard box while cleaning out my mother's house. Nana was very important to me, and a cornerstone figure in my life. I wanted to honor her by publishing her novels. I have made some necessary edits to modernize aspects of the work.

Eunice was born and raised in Oregon. She graduated from the University of California in 1924 after her family moved to Berkeley. She also spent twelve years living in Alaska. Her published books are: *Murder Breaks Trail* (1943), *Doom in the Midnight Sun* (1944), and *Murder Wears Mukluks* (1945). Among the unpublished novels *One Paw Was Red* is the fourth mystery also set in Alaska featuring her amateur detective, F. Millard Smyth. She was the "E" in Theo Durant, a group of authors, who each wrote a chapter in *The Marble Forest*, which was made into the movie *Macabre* starring Jim Backus in 1958.

Acknowledgements

I want to thank the following people who have helped me bring Dune House to life. My editor, Jim Gratiot for his patience and persistence. Laura Duffy took on the challenge of designing a series of covers for these Vintage Mysteries by Eunice Mays Boyd. Elina Cohen who designed the layout. I also want to acknowledge the very helpful guiding hand of Alan Rinzler who suggested republishing Eunice's earlier works. Special thanks also go to Eunice's nephew, Harry Watson Mays and her grandnephews John and Kirk Rademaker and their sister Erica for their support and permission to publish these novels.

About the Author

Eunice Mays Boyd (1901-1971)

Eunice was an award-winning mystery writer during the Golden Age of Agatha Christie. Her books are intelligent, cozy whodunnit murder mysteries with many twists and turns. She loved to read mysteries and prided herself in identifying the murderer well before the end. After graduating from UC Berkeley in 1924, she moved to Alaska where she lived for 12 years. Circa 1940, she returned to Berkeley where she wrote the Alaska-based F. Millard Smyth mystery series: **MURDER BREAKS TRAIL** (1943), **DOOM IN THE MIDNIGHT SUN** (1943), and **MURDER WEARS MUKLUKS** (1945). These will be republished in 2022. A fourth book in the series, **ONE PAW WAS RED** will be forthcoming (2022/2023). She co-authored **THE MARBLE FOREST** that was made into the movie "Macabre" (1958). Her new cozy murder mysteries are: **DUNE HOUSE** (11/23/2021), **SLAY BELLS** (12/7/21) and **A VACATION TO KILL** FOR (2022). These books

166

are published with her goddaughter, Elizabeth Reed Aden. **DUNE HOUSE** and **SLAY BELLS** are set in San Francisco, California and **A VACATION TO KILL FOR** is set primarily in Carcassonne, France.

Elizabeth Reed Aden

Betsy holds a doctorate degree in anthropology and has held senior executive management positions in pharmaceutical and biotech companies. She was inspired to write her own medical thriller, **THE GOLDILOCKS GENOME** (2023), by Eunice. She is finalizing a memoir, **HEPATITIS Beach** (2023/2025), about her adventures as a biomedical anthropologist living on a remote island in Melanesia where she studied the epidemiology of hepatitis B virus and how this sojourn affected her life and career. Betsy treasured and guarded the draft of A VACATION TO DIE FOR which she was given when Eunice died. In 2017 she discovered three boxes containing DUNE HOUSE, SLAY BELLS AND ONE PAW WAS RED. Eunice was an important person in her life and she is proud that she is able to share Eunice's intelligent, cleverly constructed murder mysteries from the Golden Age.

SOCIAL MEDIA HANDLES:
 Facebook: Elizabeth Reed Aden Author

Twitter: @eliz_reed_aden
Instagram: elizabeth_r_aden

AUTHOR WEBSITE:
www.elizabethreedaden.com
www.eunicemaysboyd.com

Also by Eunice Mays Boyd with Elizabeth Reed Aden

Murder Breaks Trail (1943)

Doom in the Midnight Sun (1944)

Murder Wears Mukluks (1945)

The Marble Forest (1950)

CPSIA information can be obtained
at www.ICGtesting.com
Printed in the USA
LVHW042332200423
744978LV00013B/254

9 781685 122621